# THE BALL
# LOVE CH

*A BWWM PREGNANCY ROMANCE By..*

# TASHA BLUE

# Fancy A FREE BWWM Romance Book??

Join the "**Romance Recommended**" Mailing list today and gain access to an exclusive **FREE** classic BWWM Romance book along with many others more to come. You will also be kept up to date on the best book deals in the future on the hottest new BWWM Romances.

**\* Get FREE Romance Books For Your Kindle & Other Cool giveaways**

**\* Discover Exclusive Deals & Discounts Before Anyone Else!**

**\* Be The FIRST To Know about Hot New Releases From Your Favorite Authors**

Click The Link Below To Access This Now!

## *Oh Yes! Sign Me Up To Romance Recommended For FREE!*

Already subscribed?
OK, Read On!

# Summary

After a brief fling with a famous NBA star, Layla discovered she was pregnant with his child. Terrified that he would ask for an abortion, Layla decided to raise the baby herself.

However, several months after the baby was born, Layla finally saw the errors of her ways.

She knew it was now time to tell the father the truth and so she picked up the phone and began to dial his number. Completely unaware that life as she knew it was never going to be the same again...

## Copyright Notice

# Contents

# *Chapter1*

Every time she looked at him, she couldn't help but to get a bit lost in his eyes. They were the purest shade of green she'd ever seen on a human. It made her wonder if all the magazines, sports, and entertainment media were right. That he really wasn't all that human. Dominique Johnson was magnificent on the court and Layla could luckily say he was magnificent off the court as well.

"I know you mentioned you wanted to come here for coffee one night. I hope I didn't take you out of the way or anything."

His voice was deep and velvety smooth with a notable hint of a French accent in there. He slid his hand around the huge green coffee bowl, rather than a mug, that was served and took a sip. Layla always had to tell herself not to stare and to stop being so dazzled by him every time they got together. But damn if it wasn't hard. Aside from Dominique being one of the best basketball players of his time and history, he was a knockout. Completely gorgeous with his angular chin and jaw, full pink lips, and naturally mischievous smile. Not to mention his eyes and intent gaze. He always seemed as if he had something on his mind. Then, just like any other basketball player, he always had impeccable style and his wavy brown hair was artfully cropped and kept just above his broad shoulders.

"Nah, I just had to catch a train and a bus and..." Layla began to say, teasing mostly.

It worked to make him laugh, though she really did have to bust her butt to meet up with him. Layla almost cringed as she thought about the long train ride she'd have to endure to get back to Englewood. Only for Dominique would she travel from South Side all the way to Greektown.

"You know I offered to pick you up, miss secretive," he said with a small smirk.

Layla circled her finger around the lip of her mug-bowl then took a small sip. The coffee was just as good as she'd imagined. The Bean, a popular beverage bar in Chicago, had rave reviews from all over and she'd always figured it was one of the few famous places she could actually afford to try. It kind of sucked living in one of the best cities in the U.S. and not being able to experience all it had to offer.

"So how was practice yesterday?" she asked him, hoping to change his train of thought before he got to questioning her about where she lived and whatnot.

Layla would be mortified if Dominique knew how low on the totem pole she was, especially compared to him. It was a miracle their paths even crossed in the first place.

"The coach was trying to kill us. I think he had a bad night or something. Then some of the vets on the team were pissing him off, pulling prima donna acts and whatnot. He had us running drills and plays until the assistant coaches told him to let us go home."

He shook his head with a sigh and leaned back in his seat. They had chosen a pretty secluded table in the far back of the restaurant and Dominique was sporting a hoodie and jeans. Seeming pretty clandestine so that no one would bother him too much for autographs and such. It was honestly a shock for Layla, the first time they went out, how much attention he drew. She knew he was famous and knew he had fans, but she wasn't prepared for the real life response he got when out in public.

"You guys can't just leave if you get too dead tired?" she asked him curiously.

He snorted and sat forward a bit.

"I wish; we'd get fined or benched if we did." Layla watched him a moment as he fiddled with his coffee mug. "How was your night?" he asked softly and reached forward to brush a strand of hair behind her ear.

Every time he did those little gestures of affection her entire chest flooded with warmth. She knew she'd have to staunch her intense reactions to him soon. Or else he could easily worm his way into her heart and leave her worse for wear if their relationship didn't work out. But after a month of seeing each other, she was hoping they'd make it past the fling mark.

"It was uneventful. I had a late shift at work and… then I went home," she said lamely.

She had to deal with drunk, late night customers at the diner and could barely sleep once she got off of work. But she had caught a second wind when getting ready to see Dominique; he was her escape from reality and one of the few things that kept her sane. She glanced away from him briefly, clamping down on that line of thinking. It was just what would make her a goner when it came to Dominique. He's just a regular guy with a good job, just a regular guy… it was a silent mantra she adopted early on when they started seeing each other.

"That was definitely anticlimactic," he chuckled, bringing Layla's attention back to him.

"Well, that's me sometimes," she said with a short laugh.

He gave her a wry smile and stared at her almost curiously for a moment.

"So uh… I was thinking about us and all…" His tone changed, got all serious, and Layla's spine straightened as her heart sunk. She should have never hoped… he *was* Dominique Johnson after all.

"Yeah?" she asked while looking away from his green eyes. She focused on his neck and braced herself for the inevitable.

"We've been having fun, you and I, but I think we're better off being friends from here on out."

Layla took a deep breath and almost rolled her eyes as she glanced to the right out at the rest of the tavern-like space. People were all going about their lives, talking, keeping to themselves, what have you. She wondered if her coffee would have been better had she gotten it without Dominique's company after all. Hell, she'd been so excited to go out with him that she barely tasted her coffee. She glanced down at it and was sure she would find the dark roast sour should she take another sip.

"Okay…" she said on a deep exhale.

"I don't want you to feel like this was a… hit it and quit it situation. You can call me to hang out just like always. I do enjoy your company."

Layla looked up as his accent became more pronounced. He was looking at her intently and with some remorse in his gaze.

"You don't like breaking things off with people, do you?" she asked him.

"No and it sucks all the more because of… who I am," he sighed heavily.

She should have found his words to be a little conceited, but they were true. Being dumped by a gorgeous basketball star hurt so much worse than being dumped by the okay guy who worked at the nearby pharmacy.

"It was a good month anyway," Layla murmured as she pushed away her coffee mug. "Look, I have a long ride back home…" She got up and he stood with her.

"I can give you a ride, no problem," he offered.

"No, it's fine Dom… I'll, uh, see you on TV I guess."

She chuckled then walked away from him as fast as she could. She couldn't deny that her chest felt like a pile of rocks had been dumped into it. He didn't go after her, nor did she expect him to. He probably just sat there and slowly finished his coffee. Layla took deep breaths as she made her way to the bus stop. It was freezing outside; there was hardly a fall in Chicago anymore. Only freezing wind season until the snow started up on top of the wind.

As Layla sat in the bus stop enclosure, she wondered what it would be like to live on the West Side and drive a nice car, or not even a nice car. Any car would do—a Honda Civic maybe. Or actually, she wouldn't even need a car since everything was pretty much walking distance. Maybe she could live with her cousin Tony and help him out until he got back on his feet. The bus pulled up and Layla hurried to get out of the cold. She swiped her bus pass and found a seat near the front. By the time she'd get home, she would only have a few hours to sleep before she had to get to work.

When she made it to her train and found a good window seat, she let herself doze in and out for a little while.

"Excuse me?"

Layla was roused by a gentle voice and glanced up to see a woman around her age pointing to the empty seat across from her. "Is it all right if I sit here?" she asked politely.

"Yeah, sure; you didn't have to ask," Layla said with a small chuckle.

"Last time I sat in a perfectly empty seat, some guy across form me nearly bit my head off. Said he was saving it for someone. So since then on I ask," she said as she settled in across from her.

Layla briefly took in the woman's soft pretty features and fair skin. Her blonde hair was pulled up into a bun and she wore scrubs and a pair of comfortable sneakers.

"So how's your morning going?"

Layla glanced across at the friendly woman and gave a small shrug.

"Oh, you know… it's going," she sighed.

"I completely understand that sigh," the woman chuckled. "Don't worry; if your day is bad it can only get worse and then… better." Her tone was optimistic and Layla appreciated that. It wasn't every day a stranger made another stranger feel better.

"Thanks, that actually helps." Layla laughed.

Just then a man passed by, almost falling over into the empty aisle seat next to Layla as the train met a small bump. His newspaper went flying and she helped him gather it up. Of course her eyes went right to the front page of the sports section. Dominique "The Dom" Johnson heading another win for Chicago. She tried not to wince too noticeably as she handed the paper back to the man who thanked her and continued further back. She was reminded of her melancholy and sighed deeply, wondering how a normal person got over being dumped by a star.

When Layla's stop arrived, she waved to the nurse, whose name she learned was Jen, then got off and started her walk to the apartment. She was ready for a shower and a quick nap, though as she made her way along the four blocks to her apartment. She started to feel a bit light-headed and dizzy. She should have had some water and something to eat for breakfast. Also she figured her sleepless night was catching up to her. She got home as fast as she could, though when she made it to her floor, she found her cousin Tony sitting by her front door.

"Ton? What's up?" she said and he glanced up quickly, a wide smile spreading across his face.

"How are you dear cousin of mine?" he asked and she knew that meant he was needing a meal or a place to sleep for a few hours. Tony didn't hesitate to come by when things got real low for him, but he refused to move in with her and "mooch." He was the proudest man she'd ever known.

"I'm fine, how about *you*?" she asked as she unlocked her door and gave it a kick to push it open.

They both stepped inside her cramped space. The front room was open, the kitchen, living, and dining rooms melding into one. She had one small bedroom and bathroom toward the back of the apartment and that was that. It wouldn't have been so bad if the building wasn't so old. Everything was chipped, cracked, peeling, or rusting and Layla had to learn to ignore all that a long time ago.

"Oh you know, just taking it one step at a time. I was hoping I could grab a nap on your couch?" he asked, already making himself at home.

"Of course, don't even have to ask. You know… I *could* give you a key and you wouldn't have to wait out in the hall all the time."

Layla put her bag down on the kitchen counter. Tony merely waved away her words.

"Don't mind me; as long as you're around so that I *can* wait in the hallway," he said as he got comfortable.

Layla chewed on her bottom lip pensively as she studied Tony's rugged looking windbreaker and nearly tattered jeans. His boots were about two steps away from worse for wear and she hated that he wouldn't let her help him out. Tony was like a brother to Layla; they'd grown up together. Layla's mom raised them together after her sister died and Tony's dad having stepped out of the picture the day he was born. Layla's own mom passed away from cancer as well when she was eighteen and Tony twenty. Layla had dropped out of high school when she was seventeen to take care of her mom. She had only recently gotten her GED and was saving up with the money she made at the diner to become a physical therapist.

Tony had finished high school, but he was also in the process of saving for college, not wanting to take out any loans. He had some issues with drugs, though, after Layla's mom passed and he lost his way, until recently; ever since he's been trying to make it with as little help as possible.

"Well, I'm gonna take a nap too. Maybe we can get somethin' to eat before I go to work?" Layla asked him.

He looked up at her and nodded.

"Definitely. Wake me up when you're ready, baby girl," he murmured before resting his head against the armrest and closing his eyes.

Layla hated seeing him so thin. Tony was a handsome guy: tall and he *used* to be lean and muscled. Bright hazel eyes and always clean cut, his dark caramel skin had that healthy glow and all. Lately, though, he looked like a ghost of himself, all scruffy and thin. That's what trudging your way through the bottom did to a person. It was a hard life. Layla sighed and went ahead straight to her bed. She'd shower when she woke up.

After her nap and shower, she hesitated in waking Tony. He was deeply asleep and she wondered how much he actually got on a daily basis. She knew for a fact he was in and out of shelters each week. Sighing, she decided to simply let him sleep and bring him something from Romario's down the block. Tony loved the lasagna from there and it was a hearty meal, too. Already her afternoon was turning into a busy one. She hurried as quietly as she could out of the apartment to go pick up the food. By the time she got back, she

14

barely had enough time to eat and write a note to tell Tony where to find the food. After that, she left him her spare key and was out the door, headed for the diner.

"Layla, almost two minutes late!" Layla's boss, Mr. Joe, practically yelled across the entire dining room space.

"Mr. Joe, how could I be *almost* two minutes late?" she asked him curiously.

Mr. Joe was a frumpy old Turkish man. Usually he was like an old uncle toward Layla, other days he couldn't be bothered.

"You know that clock runs two minutes fast," he said and pointed to the old antique clock on the wall.

It read exactly one o'clock, which meant Layla was two minutes early. She simply smirked and shook her head. Mr. Joe's logic only made sense to himself.

"All right, Mr. Joe, I'll try better next time," Layla said as she hurried behind the counter to toss her things in the back. She said hi to the cooks and a few other wait staff before donning her apron and name tag.

"You have section two today, Layla. Try to work your charm, flash some cleavage. We need good tips," Mr. Joe said as he passed her to get to the back.

She chuckled and shook her head at him as she went to go take care of a couple who just sat down in her section. It seemed like

Layla brought in the late lunch crowd with her. She barely had a moment to breathe until the before dinner lull.

"How are you today, Layla?" Jackson, Mr. Joe's son, came in around four while his dad turned in for the day.

Jackson was no slouch, he was just a year older than Layla at twenty-five, and days away from getting his pharmacy degree. He often got stares from the female patrons at the diner; he was all tall dark and handsome with his Middle Eastern looks and intensity.

"Ah, tired, but good. How about you?" she asked him politely as she wiped down the counter. He ran his fingers through his hair, pulling it up into a bun as he did.

"Tired as well, but actually grateful for the break from studying. Tomorrow is my last final," he said with a tired smile. "I can't wait for them to just hand me the damn degree already." Layla chuckled along with him. "So hey, you ever figure out which regular left you those basketball tickets?"

"No, actually, but they were a great tip..." Layla said, hoping Jackson wouldn't pry too much.

She had gone with him as well as the chef to the game and they both knew Dominique had pulled her aside after the game. A customer had left her three floor seat tickets and they were right next to Chicago's bench. Dominique had glanced her direction every chance he got and she hadn't thought anything of it until he was done with his interviews and caught her just as they were leaving the court. After that, she spent a lot of nights with Dominique and practically all her days off.

"Yeah, they were… and how about your special someone?" Jackson quirked a brow at her and she simply shrugged.

"It was nothing, don't get excited." She pointed to a patron who just sat down in her section. "Gotta go."

She quickly escaped and made sure to stick to the floor until her shift was over. Walking home in near thirty-degree weather was tough, especially as her usual after-work dizzy spell crashed over her and she had to focus on every step in order to get home in one piece. Her vertigo really got to her by the time she made into the apartment and she ran all the way back to her bathroom just in time to heave up whatever was in her stomach.

"Layla, you all right?" Tony came rushing in after her, pulling her hair back for her as she heaved again.

"I'm fine… just dizzy," she breathed and got up with Tony's help to go and wash out her mouth.

"You been getting dizzy often?" he asked.

She splashed water on her face a few times and grabbed her towel to dry.

"No… Yes. I don't know… it started suddenly. Just a week or so ago." She sighed and glanced at herself in the mirror. Other than the faint bags under her light brown eyes, she looked the same. Her black, sometimes unruly, curls were pulled back into a bun from work. Same light brown skin, high cheekbones and feline features. Nothing amiss… though she knew that her mother and aunt had suffered from vertigo before being diagnosed with cancer. Maybe she should go to the doctor?

"Well, maybe you should get that checked out. All I can see right now is Aunt Martha," Tony said, thinking the same way Layla was.

She noticed that Tony had showered and changed his clothes. She hoped he'd changed his mind and maybe was considering staying with her.

"I'll make the appointment if it gets worse," she said and their gazes locked until he seemed sure she'd keep the promise.

"So I found the lasagna… Thanks, you know you didn't have to," he said on a sigh and she waved away his thanks.

"You're my brother, now quit it and tell me you're moving in," she said, putting some force in her tone so that he'd finally take her seriously.

He took a tremendous breath and let it out slowly.

"Yeah I think it's best actually… I need a solid address now that I got a good job."

He grinned at her excitedly and she gasped as her heart seemed to soar with hope.

"What's the job? Where are you working?" she asked him excitedly, turning around to look at him directly instead of through the mirror.

"Well, since I've been doing good with my rehab, and my record is getting farther and farther away from me, I was finally able to get that customer service job at Cellular. I have a uniform and everything. The manager there really gave me a break," Tony said and Layla could hear the relief and happiness in his voice, not to mention the hope.

That life on the streets wasn't it for him, that things could get better and it made Layla want to cry. It had taken Tony so long to start pulling his life together. It was hard for the both of them ever since Layla's mom got sick.

"I'm so happy for you Tony!" she squealed and gave him a huge hug.

"Yeah, which means I can move in with you and pull my weight. Anything you need, if you want to split utilities and stuff I can."

"Well, really that's all included in the rent. We can go half and half; it's pretty cheap. But I want you to get your first paycheck and keep it for yourself before you chip in. Start a savings or something. Those are always good to have," Layla said.

Tony chuckled and wrapped his arm around her waist as they walked from the bathroom.

"Yeah, when I get my first paycheck you gotta help me get all of that set up," he chuckled.

"So what's your job specifically? Will you be answering phones?"

"Yeah, pretty much. It's a good gig. I could probably get us a bigger apartment, too. They pay a good wage," Tony said, his eyes brighter than Layla's seen in a while.

"First things first, though—actually do a good job at work," she chuckled.

"Right, right. Can't get too ahead of myself." He sighed and Layla savored the moment; it was the best mood she'd seen Tony in in a while.

"All right, I'm going to take a longish shower and then relax a little," Layla said.

"Do you want me to whip up some of your favorite soup?" he asked and stepped into the kitchen to pull out a can of Campbell's tomato soup.

"That sounds amazing, and some grilled cheese too?" Layla grinned at him as he got out the pot and griddle.

"Way ahead of you, baby girl."

He winked at her before she went to go take her shower and change into something more comfortable. She laid down on the couch to chat with Tony while he made dinner, dozing in and out.

Every time she got too deep into sleep, images of Dominique would bombard her. Mostly of their nights together; those would be the hardest to forget about. He was certainly no slouch in bed. Layla tried to fill her head with other things to try and push Dominique from her mind, like being happy for Tony. Wondering if she should really make a doctor's appointment or not.

"So what's up with you? Other than the diner...?" Tony knew she was seeing someone, but he didn't know who.

"You know... same old, just saving up. Hopefully I can start school by next year," Layla said on a yawn.

"Yeah, and what about that guy you've been seeing? Or girl, it's not like you share much about your private life," he said and Layla rolled her eyes, drawing a chuckle from him.

"We... well, he ended things. He was out of my league anyway," she said truthfully and Tony looked pissed almost instantly.

"Any guy would be lucky as shit to get your attention. He didn't know what he had, is all."

He spoke adamantly and Layla had to smile. That was Tony, her big brother more than he was her cousin.

"Yeah, he has too much going on anyway. I'm sure he needs someone who's more ... on his level," Layla reiterated and Tony simply shook his head.

"Don't underestimate yourself. I don't want to hear all that," he said gruffly.

Layla smiled at her cousin as he set out two bowls of soup and a plate of grilled cheese for the both of them. They ate in relative silence, Layla not in the mood to say much as her morning was weighing on her more and more. After dinner and watching a few episodes of *House of Cards* with Tony, Layla went to bed. Mostly she tossed and turned; it was impossible for her to sleep, it seemed. For one, she was way too warm, and the other, her dreams were ready to bombard her with Dominique every time she closed her eyes.

Come morning she figured she'd see Tony off on his first day, but as soon as she got out of bed, the vertigo started up with a vengeance. She barely had time to get to the bathroom before dinner from the night before was coming up.

Tony burst into the bathroom, seeming anxious. "Hey, hey! Layla, you gotta see a doctor, even if it's just a stomach bug."

"I will, I'll make an appointment, try to get in before work…" Layla said.

She didn't look at Tony until she had brushed her teeth. Then she noticed him all dressed up in khaki pants, his blue work shirt and black shoes.

"Aw, Tony…" she said and he scratched his freshly-shaved cheek. No more scruffy Tony. He had even given himself a bit of a haircut.

"Yeah, yeah… first day and all. I wanna make a good impression. Let Mr. Talbot know he wasn't wrong in going out on a limb for me."

"You'll do great. Remember, you're smart. And I believe in you," Layla said and gave him a huge hug before sending him on his way, with his own key in hand.

"Make sure you at least make an appointment for the doctor," Tony said in all seriousness before he left.

Layla promised that she would. After he was gone, she called her primary care's office, but they were booked until the following week. She really didn't feel like going to a clinic or anything either. Layla hoped it was just a mild stomach bug and prayed for it to go away soon. It wasn't like she was operating heavy machinery anyways.

For breakfast she had saltines and chicken broth. Before going to work that afternoon, she made sure to have a ginger ale and plain bread, though the bug wasn't getting any better as she walked to the diner.

She passed by the usual paper and magazine stand on the way to work and had to backtrack as she caught Dominique's handsome face splashed on the cover of several magazines. His picture looked rugged: he was sporting a five o'clock shadow and his hair was disheveled as he walked hand and hand with who the magazines identified as *Isabelle Roland*. Layla picked off one of the magazines and flipped to the article, bypassing what the cover said.

"It can't be...?" Layla read the article.

It stated that "Dominique Jones, famous basketball star, has gotten back together with his long time on and off girlfriend, Isabelle." They were seen holding hands in the West Side of Chicago just the day before. Layla put the magazine back and slowly walked away. Her expression one of disbelief and her chest felt really hot and sort of like she had heart burn.

"I guess what they say about the stars are true..." she mumbled to herself. "Never date them."

She shook her head to herself and hurried to work before she was "almost" two minutes late again.

"Layla... I never thought it possible but... you look green," Mr. Joe said as Layla was tying on her apron and stepping up behind the counter. She almost rolled her eyes and went with the amused laugh at his slightly-racist comment.

"Mr. Joe, I'm not *that* dark am I?" she asked and he began to stutter, backtracking as he realized what he said.

"No, no, I just mean you look ill, did you get something to make you sick?" he asked, his accent thicker than normal.

Layla giggled for real then and patted Mr. Joe on the back reassuringly.

"It's all right Mr. Joe, I was only teasing you a little. And I think I might have a little something. But I'm well enough to work."

Layla held her breath as Mr. Joe mulled that over for a moment. He took a deep breath that already sounded apologetic.

"Layla… you know I can't let you work if you have something catching," he said and she sighed deeply.

"All right…"

Layla knew Mr. Joe was only doing the right thing. But it meant she would go without pay until she got back to work and that she couldn't have. Layla slowly made her way back home, she stopped at the pharmacy for some antacids and passed by the feminine product aisle. She wondered briefly when the last time was that she had her period. Her jaw fell slack when she realized that she missed her period the previous month and it was going on week six without anything. With her heart racing, she grabbed a bottle of Tums and a home pregnancy test. She was hoping like hell that she only had a mere stomach flu and that was that. So many possibilities flew through her mind at the thought of having a baby.

Everything centered around money and how she wasn't even remotely ready to bring another human being into the world and raise them on her own. As she hurried into her apartment, she briefly entertained the possibility of telling Dominique about the baby, should there be one. He had just gotten back into what seemed like a complicated relationship with a world famous singer, for Pete's sake. Layla didn't want that kind of stress in her child's life… again, *should* there be one. She hurried into the bathroom and locked the door, and sat down on the edge of the tub to read the pregnancy test with shaking hands.

Layla took several deep breaths to try and calm herself before she followed the directions. After she was done with the bathroom, she set the test aside carefully and set a timer on her cell phone. She really tried not to sit and stare at the time go by, but she couldn't force herself to stay away and occupy herself. Layla instead chewed on Tums while staring at the timer. When the clock flashed at zero and the alarm sounded, Layla felt as if her body was shutting down. She wasn't ready to see the results, mostly because she had this gut feeling. Ever since she realized that she was late for her period, she knew.

"Oh God…" She took a huge breath and picked up the pregnancy test. Clear as day there were two little positive red lines. "Holy shit…" She nearly collapsed onto the floor. Her hands began shaking and she was sure a panic attack was coming for her.

"Layla…? Lay, you home?" Tony must have seen her bag. She checked the time and briefly wondered if he'd get off so early in the afternoon every day or if he was on a lunch break. "Today was training day so they sent me home early to study up on proper customer service and whatnot… Are you here?" His voice neared the bedroom and she forced herself into a standing position. He poked his head into the room and immediatcly took note of her wide eyes and pale face.

"What happened? You look like you saw a ghost." Tony hurried in and made to take Layla's hands. That's when he saw it. "Is this a pregnancy test...?" He was mostly talking to himself as he took it and read the results. He got really quiet then and sat heavily on Layla's bed.

"I... I don't have the stomach flu... or cancer," she whispered.

"You're having a baby." Tony's tone was blunt and shock was heavy in his voice as well.

"I'm gonna be an unclc?" He glanced up at Layla's face and she nodded slowly, woodenly. "Shit, I'm gonna be an uncle..."

"How am I supposed to take care of this baby, Tony?"

Layla's voice was broken with restrained emotion. She was really trying to keep it together, meanwhile her insides felt as if they were in turmoil.

"Just like our moms took care of us for as long as they could. Plus, you'll have me. I'll help you. That baby won't grow up without a father figure. Promise." Tony's words were sincere and his gaze never left Layla's. She was a bit soothed that she wasn't *completely* alone. "But now you really have to make a doctor's appointment," he said sternly.

"Yeah, I will… I'm just in shock still," she mumbled.

"Here, why don't you sit down out here and I'll get you a ginger ale?" he offered. She couldn't help her fond smile as she nodded and let him lead her into the living room. "So, uh… if you don't mind me asking…?" Tony glanced over his shoulder at Layla curiously.

"If I tell you, you'd freak out," she warned him.

"Why? Is it Jackson? You know he's not all that bad of a guy."

Layla laughed, she wished it were Jackson.

"I don't think having the father in the baby's life will do any good. It'd make things way too complicated." Layla sighed.

With how much media that followed Dominique, if he wasn't careful, she knew she'd probably surface as some money-grubbing fling that wouldn't go away if she contacted him about the baby. Dominique had been her first sort of relationship in years, there was no doubt in her mind that he was the dad. Still, she didn't exactly feel like fueling certain stereotypes. Not when she could give a shot at raising her baby with a somewhat normal life. She just really needed to get into school already, take up more shifts at the diner, and take Tony up on moving into a better apartment.

So many things ran through her mind as everything started to truly shift. Giving the baby up was out of the option—she wasn't raised that way and she wouldn't turn her back on family no matter how hard life would be for her until she got a good job and a place away from the South Side.

"So you're definitely not going to tell him? Like at all?" Tony asked, Layla could tell he was hiding his incredulity. "Even my dad knew I existed, at least he had the choice of not being in my life," he pointed out.

"Maybe I'm like my mom in that way. Maybe I know that if a man doesn't want me, he certainly won't want a baby. Anyway, things would be so much easier if he doesn't know. You just have to trust me on that."

Tony gave Layla a long look, sighed, and then nodded his head.

"All right, if you really and truly think it's best. Don't worry, baby or no baby, things are going to start looking up for us. You're starting school soon, and I've got a good job I'm not going to let slip away from me." Tony walked over and gave Layla a kiss on the forehead. "We've got each other's backs," he said softly.
Layla took a deep breath and she nodded, knowing that no matter how optimistic Tony was, there would definitely be a few bumps along the road.

# *Chapter 2*

*One Year Later*

LJ wouldn't stop crying. Every time he got even remotely hungry, he let heaven, hell, and everywhere in between know it.

"I know, I know, baby, the bottle is taking too long to warm up…" Layla murmured as she bounced her two-month-old on her hip. LJ was normally the happiest baby on the planet, though when it came to his food, there was no messing around.

"Someone's hungry." Tony came home in the nick of time.

"Oh thank *God*. Please, do your little dance with him. He won't calm down."

Layla's voice was filled with exasperation and exhaustion. She hadn't slept since the baby was born.

"I heard him crying all the way down the hallway," Tony said as he put his messenger bag down and went to take Lucas.

As soon as he saw his uncle, his cries quieted a bit and soon stopped altogether as Tony sang him the silly "feeding time" song he came up with a few weeks ago. Layla was really happy she had Tony when she did. She wasn't sure she and Lucas would have made it just the two of them.

"So we need to talk about some things, Layla… I have good news and bad news."

Tony spoke in a light tone, but Layla learned to dread those words over the course of her life. The "we need to talk" phrase never led to anything good.

"What's the bad news?" she asked as she checked LJ's bottle.

It was finally the perfect temperature. She turned off the stove and handed the bottle to Tony who started to feed LJ right away.

"Good news is I think I found a place that we can afford. It's bigger, in a better neighborhood… bad news is that it's in another state… where my job wants me to transfer to for a promotion."

Tony stared at Layla for her to respond in any way. She was holding the saucepan of hot water over the sink and stuck between wanting to congratulate Tony and urging him to take the promotion. And the realization that the in-between of them moving to another state and getting settled would be beyond stressful, and frankly, Layla was nearly at her cap.

"That's great that they're promoting you… to what position though?" she asked and held in her sigh as she poured the water out and rinsed the pot.

"To customer service supervisor. One of their offices in Maryland could use someone like me to help improve their numbers.

They'd pay to move us out there and all. The perks are pretty good," he said with a small smile.

"Well, of course you *have* to take the job, Tony. That's out of the question," Layla said, trying to sound happy for him, though all she felt was weary and lethargic.

"I was thinking that maybe you could apply to one of the schools over there and we can… you know, be on our way and stuff."

Layla knew Tony's plan sounded good and she was all for it.

"So you'd have to go ahead to Maryland first and then we'd move out there with you?" she asked him and he nodded.

"Yeah, it would only be up to a month tops before things get settled to where I can fly you both out…" Tony said. "Do you think you can manage with him for that long? I can give you some money for a baby sitter for when you have to work at the diner," he offered.

"Sure, yeah, we can figure something out. Are you going to be here the rest of the night?" Layla asked him, sleep heavy on her mind.

"Of course, go and take a nap."

Tony sent Layla to her room and she met unconsciousness with open arms as soon as her body hit the bed.

Tony woke her some time later with LJ lying on her belly right in front of her face. He smiled happily, with his one dimple in his left cheek and pushed himself up to give her a sloppy open mouthed kiss on the cheek. Layla smiled and sat up, taking LJ into her arms.

"You slept a little past your alarm, but you shouldn't be late," Tony said and Layla's eyes widened as she glanced around for her phone.

"It's tomorrow already?" she said in shock and Tony chuckled.

"Yeah, it's Saturday. Take a breath, you'll be on time," he reassured her.

"Okay… are you sure you don't mind watching him weekends? I hate taking up all your spare time like this," Layla said as she kissed Lucas on the top of the head and laid him back down on the bed.

"Don't even start with that. I made a promise didn't I? Plus, Luc and I need our guy time."

Layla glanced down at Lucas who was chewing on one of his toys and grinning up at her. He really was the cutest baby on earth. He had his father's green eyes, light caramel colored skin, and a head full of soft dark brown curls. Layla left LJ with his uncle; she hated that they literally created new working schedules to complement each other's so that someone was always with Lucas. Mostly she hated it because she felt she was taking Tony's life away from him. Soon though, she wouldn't even have Tony to babysit and that worried her. She didn't know that she could trust just anyone to watch Lucas, even if he was relatively easy.

"Okay, I'll be back later!" Layla called over her shoulder as she rushed out to get to work. She was grateful she saw Jackson manning the counter instead of Mr. Joe. He'd definitely give her a lecture on being four minutes late.

"Hey Layla how are you?" Jackson greeted her with a bright smile as she hurried to get her stuff put away and grab her apron.

"I'm all right… Slow tonight?" She glanced around for the first time and realized that the diner was surprisingly sparse.

"Yeah, it is… I've actually been applying for jobs in the last two hours," he said. After Jackson got his degree and license he'd been looking for a pharmacy job, but the best opportunities for him were far from South Side or in other states. His main hindrance was not wanting to leave his dad to handle the diner alone.

"Any luck with something close to town?" Layla asked him and he shook his head.

"I don't know… my dad doesn't want to be a burden on me so he's thinking of selling the diner."

Layla's jaw dropped as a flurry of thoughts crossed her mind.

"He's seriously thinking about it?" she asked and Jackson nodded slowly.

"He's gotten offers from both IHOP and Denny's for the building, the location. He's trying to see if they're still interested," Jackson said without much concern, as if his father weren't considering a potentially life-altering decision.

"What about… us?" Layla asked curiously.

"Of course you all would keep your jobs with whoever moves in. But management would change and, of course, policies and such. No one would be out of a job," he said reassuringly. "So how's Baby Lucas?" he asked.

Layla nodded.

"He's fine, happy as ever…" she said on a sigh.

She couldn't help the solid knot that settled in her gut. She didn't like the sound of Mr. Joe selling the diner around the same time Tony would be leaving her and LJ for a while.

"Don't worry about the diner Layla. If anything, my dad wouldn't sell unless he was sure everyone was taken care of," Jackson noted Layla's expression and reassured her again.

"All right… I just can't help but worry," she admitted.

"My mother used to say that when I was young, before my dad bought the diner. That she couldn't help but worry. But things never were uncertain for long. Just have faith." He smiled at Layla and went to go talk to the cook in back.

Layla sighed and simply manned the counter, keeping it clean for no one in particular. It was the slowest Saturday Layla ever experienced at the diner. She was counting on weekend tips to buy groceries before her paycheck cleared.

After her shift, she slowly walked back home, kicking rocks and playing with figures and dates in her mind. She had to buy Lucas' formula and diapers, that was a given. The rest she'd have to wing it until the following Friday or owe Tony for Friday. It seemed like she'd have to owe Tony yet again for groceries when that was supposed to be her expense.

"Mommy's home!" Tony said in his baby talk which got a resounding happy squeal from LJ.

A smile was put on Layla's face almost instantly when she saw Lucas reaching for her, a big dimpled smile on his face.

"There's my little man."

She smiled and scooped him up out of his play chair. She had a suspicion that he'd be walking sooner than most babies. Lucas started babbling right away and Layla tried her best to indulge him in a conversation about his day.

"So, uh… Luc and I went out for a walk today and passed by the magazine stand. It was the weirdest thing. He saw a picture of… uh, Dominique Johnson and pointed at the magazine. He actually fussed until I picked it up so he could see it better."

Tony paused, looking at Layla expectantly and she held her breath waiting for him to continue. She had told Tony who LJ's father was, but he respected her decision not to tell Dominique and didn't push her on the subject after she left Dominique's name off of LJ's birth certificate.

"He's engaged to Isabelle, it's all over... everywhere," Tony said apologetically.

Layla wished he didn't feel the need to be apologetic or tiptoe around the subject of Dominique.

"So you think LJ recognized him?" Layla asked.

Tony laughed and shook his head.

"No, he just wanted something to chew on. I left his toys by accident."

Layla glanced down at LJ who was playing with her hair and trying to put it into his mouth.

"Do you think..." she paused to take a deep breath and sat down on the couch. "Do you think I should tell Dom about LJ?" Layla asked Tony, who was already nodding vigorously.

"I understand where you're coming from and all, with not wanting to make LJ's life so hectic. But I think that Dominique should know and you should give LJ a chance to know his dad. It's... really, it's not fair for you to choose that for him."

Layla sighed deeply and glanced down at LJ who was then dozing off.

"Yeah… I was thinking that, too. But I mean, Tony, we aren't in the best of situations right now and I don't want to look like I'm after his money," Layla said slowly. "Nor do I want him to think about taking custody or something horrible like that."

"You dated him right? Even if for a little while. Do you think he'd do something like that?"

Layla shrugged, in all honestly, their relationship was mostly sexual.

"I mean, he doesn't seem like a bad guy from what I've seen on TV and such." Tony shrugged.

Layla rubbed her temples and sighed.

"Mr. Joe might be selling the diner…"

"*What*?" Tony startled LJ and Layla soothed him while Tony stood up and began pacing. "What does that mean? Why would he sell? Will everyone lose their jobs?" Tony asked anxiously.

"Jackson assured me that we wouldn't, but I'm not sure. I do have a bad feeling, though."

"Don't worry, soon I'll be heading to Maryland to get things set up for us."

Tony and Layla talked more about his work plans; he'd be leaving at the end of the week and wanted to make sure Layla and LJ were okay while he was gone. She knew that if she were going to go through with telling Dominique about LJ, it'd have to be before they left the state at least.

"Should LJ be teething already? He likes chewing on everything."

Tony distracted Layla from her thoughts. They were sitting on the floor of the living room, flipping through Netflix. LJ was wide awake and reaching for some toys on the floor, trying to perfect his floor wiggling skills.

"Well, some babies start as early as three months, he's just about three months so I'd say it's normal." Layla shrugged.

"So… when are you gonna call him then?" Tony asked in a slightly bored tone, but Layla could tell he was really curious for her answer.

"I'm still gearing myself up to do it… he could have changed his number you know, then I'd have no way to contact him, really."

"Don't end the mission before you've even started; just call him."

Tony urged Layla to pull out her phone and at least pull up Dominique's contact. She glanced at LJ, who rolled onto his back and was staring at her upside down. Before she could second-guess herself, she dialed the number and put the phone to her ear. It rang about ten times before Layla got Dominique's voice mail. The only real confirmation that she had called Dominique was when the automated voice switched to Dominique's voice stating his name briefly and carrying on with the automated message.

Layla realized that she'd either soon have to hang up or leave a message. Her heart rate jumped even higher than it already was. She only hesitated briefly after the beep sounded for her to leave her message.

"Hey… Dominique, it's Layla, from like… a year ago we saw each other for little over a month. Um… I really need to speak with you about something important so get back to me when you can. My number is the same by the way… okay, bye."

She hung up and glanced over at Tony who was holding his breath and trying not to laugh. Layla rolled her eyes at him and threw one of the couch cushions, making LJ crack up when it hit Tony in the head.

"I'm sorry, but that sounded so painfully awkward," Tony chuckled.

"Well, how would *you* react in my situation?" she shot back at him and he held his hands up in surrender.

"Okay, you're right, I'm sorry…" Tony apologized, though he still had a smirk on his face.

"Do you think he'll call back?" Layla asked slowly.

"Well… I mean, you didn't exactly mention the word 'baby' so… who knows. If he's a good guy, he would call back… if he checks his own messages," Tony sighed.

"Wouldn't basketball players check their messages? Like, what if their mom calls them?" Layla asked.

"Well, okay, yeah. But I wouldn't have mentioned that the two of you had a thing a year ago. Any guy would be wary of a woman calling from a short relationship more than two months later."

"Well, exactly, he'd *have* to think that there's a baby related issue to make me call him," Layla said.

"He did just get engaged, too…" Tony said.

Layla sighed in frustration.

"Tony please, I'm already regretting calling him in the first place," she said.

"All right, all right, I'm sorry… so what are we watching?" he asked.

"Umm… LJ what do you want to watch?"

Layla looked down at Lucas who was busy chewing on one of his rattlers.

"I'm guessing he doesn't mind too much," Tony said and chose a random movie, when Layla realized he chose *Minions* she turned into a little kid, watching almost as raptly as Lucas was.

About halfway through the movie, her cell phone rang loudly, jolting Layla and Lucas from the movie, though Tony stayed asleep.

41

Layla glanced down at the screen of her phone and her heart nearly seized up when she saw it was Dominique calling back. She slowly grabbed her phone and answered it, making sure Lucas was quiet before she connected the call.

"Layla... hey, I just got out of practice and caught your message."

He sounded a bit anxious and she felt pity for him and shame for herself for what she was about to tell him.

"Yeah, I have, um... something to talk to you about," she said softly and heard him take a deep breath on the other line.

"Is it medical...?" he asked slowly and LJ complained as Layla had paused the movie and wasn't paying him much attention.

"In a manner of speaking... um, I had a baby, Dominique— your baby," she said the words in a rush and was met with a very eerie silence.

"Is that... is that the baby in the background? Wait, are you *sure*?" Dominique's words came out in a rush and his accent thickened considerably.

"You're the only one I had been with in a while, Dominique... and I—I know I should have told you earlier. But I didn't want all that stress in the baby's life. I realized, though, that I can't just deny Lucas his father..." Layla spoke in a rush, unsure any of what she said made sense.

"The baby's name is Lucas?" Dominique asked in a choked voice.

"Yes… and I understand if you want to do a paternity test. That's if you want to be in his life," she said hastily. Layla felt as if her words were coming out all wrong.

"I'm sorry, Layla, I'm having trouble with this right now. *Why* wouldn't you have told me, regardless of what you think might happen, before the baby was born? Don't you think that if I had a child I'd want to be there from the very beginning?"

Layla was unprepared for his sudden anger and she took pause.

"Dominique, I—I know I made a bad decision, but I'm calling you now…" she said lamely, trying to go for the "put the past behind us" route.

"Where do you live? I want to see him and you're right, I want a paternity test," he said in a measured tone.

"Dominique…"

"I can't talk anymore, just send me the address and I'll be on the way as soon as you do," he said crisply and ended the call.

Layla closed her eyes and exhaled deeply. LJ was staring up at her with his wide green eyes and long lashes. He knew something was up and touched her face as he made a small inquiring sound.

"Everything is fine, little man, don't worry… you'll be meeting your daddy soon." She smiled at him and he smiled back, happy and completely oblivious. Layla took a deep breath and shifted Lucas in her arms to text Dominique her address, cringing as she thought of him showing up to her rundown place. She followed up her text with a very polite request, asking him to come by in the morning. All he sent back was a resounding, "K."

"Dammit."

Layla sighed and pressed play on the movie. Her stomach was in knots and she felt like throwing up a little. Layla glanced at sleeping Tony and poked him with her toe.

"Tony!" she hissed at him and LJ's head swung over to his uncle.

He actually babbled in Tony's direction to wake him up, too.

"What… what?" he murmured and slowly opened his eyes.

"He called back… Dominique… he could come by tonight or tomorrow morning," she said with veiled panic.

Tony's eyes widened and he sat up abruptly.

"Shit, seriously? What'd he say?" Tony glanced down at the phone in Layla's hand and LJ who was being quite vocal. "Why didn't I hear any of this?"

"He was mad, upset that I didn't tell him from the start," Layla said, her chest constricting a little as she thought about facing him in a matter of hours. Whether it was when the sun came up or that night. "He wants to do a paternity test and really wants to see Lucas, of course." Layla was starting to feel the gravity of her decision to not tell Dominique about Lucas earlier, like when she was pregnant with him.

"I think he might hate me... and take Lucas," she said and Tony shook his head adamantly.

"No, he wouldn't do that. Lucas is still breast feeding," Tony pointed out.

"Babies drink formula, Lucas does too, that doesn't really matter," Layla said, already getting a lot stressed out and regretting her decision to tell Dominique.

"Don't freak out. I'm sure it won't be as bad as you think after he calms down some," Tony tried to reassure her, but she was quickly surpassing the threshold of being able to calm down.

"I have to take a walk... or something, I need air," Layla said and stood up with Lucas.

"But what if he comes by tonight?" Tony asked.

"I asked him to come by tomorrow morning and he said, 'K,'" Layla said as she got up with Lucas.

"All right I'll come with you then," Tony said.

They completely forgot about the movie and simply put on shoes and jackets to get out into fresh air.

"I don't know… I just think I'll puke or something if I see him tomorrow and he's still angry," Layla said while pushing Lucas' stroller.

His big eyes were riveted on the full moon over Layla's shoulder.

"Layla, I've got your back no matter what."

Tony gave her a swift hug and she drew some comfort that she at least had a Tony by her side. After their walk, Layla took care of Lucas, bathing him, feeding him, and putting him to bed. For the most part, she watched Lucas sleep until the sun started to rise; only then did she doze off for a bit.

"Layla… Layla, wake up." She was roused by Tony's quiet and urgent whisper. Layla opened her eyes, her gaze going right across to Luca's crib. He was still sound asleep.

"What is it?" she asked groggily.

She sat up and almost squealed when she saw Dominique towering just inside the doorway to her bedroom. His eyes were riveted on LJ.

"He looks almost just like me… when I was a baby."

Dominique's voice was hoarse and he looked rougher than Layla had ever seen him, as if he hadn't slept and just threw on some sweats to hurry over at the crack of dawn. Tony rocked back and forth on his heels briefly and then squeezed out of the room. Layla got out of bed, thankful that she wore something other than short

46

shorts and a tank top with no bra. Though wearing short shorts and an oversized sweater wasn't too much of a step up.

"How old is he?" Dominique asked without looking over at Layla. He stepped closer to Lucas's crib and reached out to touch one of his sock clad feet.

"Nearly three months... a week off," Layla said in a voice barely above a whisper. Dominique had to duck even when he was fully in the room.

"And his name is... Lucas?" Dominique looked over at her then, his eyes were red, but there were no tears. Layla simply nodded and held her breath when a ghost of a smile touched Dominique's lips. "My grandfather's name is Lucas... he's one of the best men I know—" Dominique got choked up as he stared down at Lucas. Layla couldn't believe the display she was witnessing, she had no idea how exactly Dominique would react. But she expected some anger, indignation, *something*. But he was emotional, he looked... happy as he gazed down at Lucas.

"It's just... there's so many things, so many stories you hear about having your first child. I always wanted a boy first and I wanted to name him Lucas. Then... I walk in here and I *know* he's mine. I can feel it. There's no doubt..." Dominique fell silent as he was overcome with emotion and Layla couldn't help but get choked up herself.

"I'm sorry Dominique… I'm so sorry I didn't tell you," she said in a shaky voice.

"I understand why you did it. I don't blame your reasoning, but I'm glad you decided to finally tell me, while he's still young." Dominique took a deep steadying breath and he glanced around briefly.

"Sorry you can't really stand up straight. The place is kind of small…"

"To say the least. You can't live here… this is—when he starts walking he'll be into everything. *Everything* looks like it's chipping off in this place."

Dominique's voice had begun to rise and Luca stirred unhappily in his sleep. Both their gazes locked onto Lucas. Layla hoped he would stay asleep; if he woke up early he'd be tired and cranky all day. But of course he woke up, wide eyed and stared directly into Dominique's eyes.

"He even has my eyes…" He laughed and then slowly reached down to pick Lucas up.

"Oh, you still have to support his head a little, like this."

Layla stepped over to show him the right way to hold Lucas. LJ was still waking up so he simply stared at Dominique and yawned.

"He's perfect…" Dominique whispered, the biggest smile on his face.

A few tears did escape Layla's eyes then. Her chest was full of warmth as she hoped for the best possible outcome.

"I'm your papa…" He spoke to Lucas who smiled at him and reached for Dominique's hair.

"Oh, yeah, he loves you already," Layla said with a chuckle.

"Do you know any French?" he asked her and she laughed.

"No, only the very obvious words," she told him.

"Well, he's going to have to learn French; my mother wouldn't have it any other way…" Dominique said with humor in his voice.

Layla almost froze as she began to realize that Lucas was getting an entire family in having his father in his life. He wouldn't have just merely Layla and Tony in his life anymore.

"How much family do you have…?" Layla asked him. She couldn't believe she didn't get such basic information when they were seeing each other. Then, for the tenth time, she reminded herself that they hardly talked about anything too deep around all the sex they had. Just like the other times she reminded herself, she felt a faint sting. Layla was just a dalliance for him, nothing serious at all. Then Lucas happened.

"Well, my mom's family is small and they still live in France. She only has one brother and both her parents. My father, he lives here in Chicago with a much larger family. I have a bunch of cousins because he has five other siblings. Then both of his parents

49

are alive as well…" Dominique glanced around Layla's small space once again and his expression sobered.

"You only have the one cousin?" he asked in a low tone, gesturing with his chin towards the living room.

"Yeah, he's like a brother to me…" Layla told him.

"Well, how about we go for breakfast and talk about some things?" Dominique said, his tone all business.

Layla took a deep breath and tried to steel herself for the upcoming conversation.

"All right… let me just get changed, then get him changed." She sighed and moved towards her closet to grab something to wear. She changed quickly, freshened up a little in the bathroom, then hurried out to get Lucas's breakfast ready. Dominique was out in the living room talking with Tony and still holding Lucas. Layla got LJ's bag ready quickly then went over to take him from Dom. Or at least attempt to.

"I'd like to get him ready," he said, standing with LJ and looking down at Layla expectantly.

"Okay, sure. Yeah I can show you how…" she said and sent a glance to Tony who gave her a thumbs up.

"Is he usually so well behaved?" Dominique asked as he laid LJ on the bed next to the change of clothes Layla laid out for him.

"Yeah, unless he's hungry or really tired. Actually, if you're a second late in feeding him he'll act up," she said, making Dom chuckle almost fondly.

"Like father like son... man that's so... *weird*—he's just like me!"

Layla chuckled, watching as Dominique spoke to Lucas in French, also translating his words to English from time-to-time, wondering out loud if Lucas was going to be a basketball star, too.

"Does he have any basketball toys or anything like it?" Dominique asked her, glancing around in Lucas's crib.

"Oh no, he doesn't have... anything like that yet," Layla said.

Most of what Lucas had was from Goodwill, she didn't want to let Dominique on to that, though. He obviously already had a problem with Lucas staying in the apartment.

"Well, we have to get him new toys and a little hoop so he can practice his jump shots."

Layla giggled, which caused Lucas to send her a giant grin as Dom successfully changed his first diaper. Getting Lucas ready took a little longer than usual, of course; it was Dominique's first time, so that was to be expected. Layla couldn't help but love the way Dominique spoke to Lucas constantly, as if he were a little person and his son. Not just a three-month-old baby he didn't know he had. She could tell that he loved LJ already.

They passed Tony in the living room and Dominique asked if he wanted to come along.

"No, you guys do your thing, I know there's a lot you need to talk about," he said and waved them off.

Layla followed behind Dominique, who was pushing Lucas's stroller.

"So you don't have a car or car seat for him...?" Dominique asked Layla though she was sure he knew the answer already.

"I don't have a car, but we lucked out in getting that stroller, it breaks down into a car seat," Layla said.

"Oh, great then." Dominique led them to his car, it was a fancy looking Audi.

Dominique quickly figured out how to break the stroller down and fit the car seat into the backseat and rest of the stroller into the trunk. Layla smiled at Lucas who seemed to be having the time of his life, he loved being outside.

Once inside the car and actually on the road, Layla could see Dominique's mind moving at a million miles per hour. She wondered what he was thinking. What Tony said to him earlier... what would result from him finding out about Lucas.

"You're really quiet," Layla sighed as she pushed her fingers through her hair, moving it out of her face.

"Just thinking…" he murmured and took a deep breath. "I want you out of that poor excuse for an apartment."

"What do you mean…?"

"I mean as soon as we get back you're packing up your stuff and I'm going to put you and Lucas in a hotel until I can get you a house."

He spoke so frankly, as if what he said were simply *going* to happen.

"Dominique… I can't just—you can't just *buy* a…"

"I can actually. It's easy, the only work is finding one in a good neighborhood around good schools. And you don't have to worry about the money at all. I just don't want *you* and especially not Lucas living on the South Side."

Layla simply blinked at Dominique a few times; even though she shouldn't have been, she was shocked.

"Now I know why you never invited me over…" He sighed and Layla realized he was pulling into a parking lot outside of Pancake House. Even early in the morning it seemed full, their pancakes were that good.

"I didn't want you feeling sorry for me or wanting to give me a handout. That wasn't what I was after…" she said and trailed off before she got to talking about what she *was* hoping for; which was him, but that was unrealistic obviously, the man was engaged for Pete's sake.

"I don't want you to feel like a charity case, Layla. I just want to take care of Lucas and make sure you are taken care of as well." He glanced at her sincerely and they shared a small moment in the car, until Lucas spoke up, babbling loudly. "Don't worry, little man, we're getting to it." Dominique looked back at Lucas with a smile and tickled him under the chin.

They got out of the car and Layla noted how Dom immediately pulled up his hood before going about getting Lucas's stroller from the trunk. Lucas began complaining as it was taking too long to get him out of the car and Layla went to pick him up. He started sucking his thumb, letting her know he was hungry and would continue complaining until he was fed.

"I have to feed him... Did we pack a bottle?" Dominique checked the bag in the car and rummaged through it quite a bit, enough to tell Layla that they forgot Lucas's bottle. She sighed when Lucas started to cry. "I'll have to breast feed him..." she murmured and got into the backseat with LJ.

Dominique's eyes widened briefly, as he watched Layla get ready to feed LJ, he clearly was at a loss for what to do. He ended up closing the other door and standing outside awkwardly. Layla couldn't help her small chuckle before focusing on getting Lucas his breakfast.

"Are you, ah... almost done?" Dominique poked his head inside, looking anywhere but directly at Layla.

"Almost, just a few more minutes," she said and he got into the front seat, deciding to wait inside.

"Does that hurt?" he asked after a short moment of quiet.

"Sometimes, but not usually…" Layla wasn't sure how in depth she should get into the topic of breast feeding. She doubted Dominique wanted to know about her sore nipples and whatnot.

"Does he sleep through the night?"

Dom's voice was more curious than anything and again Layla was heartened by the fact that he seemed so into everything surrounding Lucas.

"He's sleeping much better now than he used to a few weeks ago. But he still has nights where he'll wake up and refuse to go back to sleep until dawn."

Layla yawned, her sleepless night creeping up on her. LJ finished feeding and she took some time to burp him.

"Will people recognize you?" Layla asked him when they finally made it from the car to the actual restaurant.

"There's always a possibility…" He shrugged slightly and held the door open for Layla and LJ's stroller.

Layla spoke to the hostess, giving her name. Dominique actually kept his head down and avoided any detection. They were brought back to their table quickly since it was just the two of them with a stroller.

"When it gets out that… you have a son, how will we be able to, like… go out?"

"The media isn't as bad as you think. They don't swarm and trap people in their homes. But should it be that big of news, I would hire security."

"I don't want LJ to have to deal with cameras flashing in his face all the time," Layla murmured.

"LJ?"

"Oh, yeah Lucas Johnson… LJ," she explained.

"Did you put my name on his birth certificate?"

Layla hesitated in answering his question, she knew it would upset him.

"I'm guessing not then." He sat back with a big sigh and pushed his hood off of his head.

"Oh my goodness, you're Dominique Johnson," Their waitress had come up just in time to see him reveal himself. She drew several eyes to their table as well with her less than discreet outburst.

"Hi, how are you?" he smiled at her politely, but Layla could see the tension in his shoulders.

"I have to say you're making my day." She laughed, clearly excited at who she was waiting on for the time being.

"Oh c'mon, I'm just a regular guy. Having breakfast," he chuckled.

Layla smirked at his subtle tell to the waitress to keep things quiet.

"Oh, oh of course. I'm sorry, it was just a shock," she said in a conspiratorial tone. "So what can I get you all to drink?" she asked, her tone bubbly.

When she finally turned her attention toward Layla and Lucas, her eyes widened slightly, but she didn't say anything. Neither did they, apart from giving her their drink orders. When she was gone, Dominique sighed deeply and glanced down at Lucas. He was playing with his bib and pacifier in happy oblivion.

"A lot of things will change…" Dominique sighed softly and caressed Lucas's soft curls.

# Chapter3

"So did you have plans to get out of the situation you were in? Other than follow Tony to Maryland, which isn't happening by the way." Dominique had about two and a half cups of coffee sent to him by Chicago Horns fans grateful for his ushering the team's last win.

"I was saving up to go to school; I want to become a physical therapist. There's this vocational school that's pretty cheap per semester. So I was simply headed toward that. But then Lucas came… and I *know* that apartment isn't the best condition to raise a baby in. When Tony gave me the news of his promotion and moving to a better apartment, I figured it was best," Layla said in a low voice.

Dom had urged her to speak quietly to lower the risk of other people overhearing.

"…you remind me of my mother. Believe it or not, I didn't grow up rich or even middle class. She worked very hard just to even feed us and help my uncle in taking care of my grandparents who are both disabled. She was also trying to save to go to school for counseling. Then my father wanted to help and he flew me to America so she could have it easier. My uncle urged her to let me go and she did. Eventually, she and my uncle made enough money to put my grandparents in a place where they could have some freedom and get the help they need. My father helped with that as well. Then she finally had enough to go to school and things have been better since. She now owns her own counselling center and takes care of my grandparents without any help."

Layla saw Dominique get a little lost in his story and she could tell he missed his family back in France.

"So… did you always know your father?" Layla asked.

"No, he visited France and met my mother by chance, they only had one night together. She didn't have any way to contact him. But he had been looking for her after their night together. He, of course, left France and eventually forgot about her. Then on another trip over he remembered their night and went back to the same street in our town. I was five by then and playing in the street when I was supposed to stay close to the walk ways. I ran right into him and mom came running out. Then they saw each other, he looked down at me, then at her… then at me again."

Layla chuckled with him and Dom took another sip of his coffee.

"Since then he's always been a part of my life. He saved us really."

Layla watched him take a bite of his pancakes and she glanced down at her own. She had barely touched her food.

"Have your parents ever… gotten together?" The question left Layla's lips before she could stop it.

"Ah, no… my father is happily married. My mother is happy with her life and dates more often than I'd like." He chuckled. "But all of that is to say… I understand your struggle and I just want to help you. As the mother of my child, it's almost a sin to simply leave you where you are." He spoke sincerely and stared into Layla's eyes intently.

She was always unnerved when he did that, his eyes were just so green.

"So let me put you and Lucas into a suite, Tony as well until he makes his move. Let me take care of you."

Layla took a deep breath and she nodded. "Okay…"

"And I want to be on his birth certificate," he added.

"Of course, yeah, we can get that taken care of," she said and reached for her cup of coffee to take a sip.

"You're tired…" he observed and Layla smirked.

"Yeah, I was up all night worrying you'd… I don't know… take Lucas away," she blurted, again without thinking.

"I wouldn't do that, Layla," he said bluntly and glanced down at Lucas, who was then dozing off into a nap. "Are you going to eat anything? You look thinner than when I last saw you," Dom said, his eyes roaming all over Layla, making her feel more than uncomfortable.

"I'm fine... I'll probably have more of an appetite after I've slept."

She tried to brush off the line of talk, but Dominique sat forward and reached out to touch her jaw, then his long fingers caressed her collar bone. She had to suppress a shiver and looked down at her plate.

"Please eat something," he said adamantly and she sighed, but didn't protest.

She cut into her huge pancakes and took a bite; as soon as the food hit her stomach, she realized how hungry she really was.

"So what about your fiancée?" Layla asked him, hoping it wasn't some sort of sensitive topic for him or anything.

She looked up at Dominique and saw him gingerly taking Lucas out of his stroller and cradling him close to his chest.

"Don't worry about her," he said softly while staring down at Lucas while he slept.

"Can you stop telling me not to worry? If she's going to be in LJ's life, I want to know she isn't some crazy person. No offense..." Layla was probably a bit harsher than she intended, but she could feel the sleep-deprived migraine coming on.

"She's going to be shocked. But I'll handle her. I wouldn't have her coming to you or LJ halfcocked. She's not crazy," he said defensively.

A small part of Layla sort of hated that he got so defensive over Isabelle, it meant he really had feelings for her. But of course he did, they were engaged.

"All right, I'm sorry…" she said and took a sip of her coffee before glancing around. Many curious eyes were on Dom as he held LJ. "Can we go…?" she asked, not liking all the attention.

"You barely ate anything," he pointed out.

"Yeah, but it's getting more crowded," she said and he glanced around briefly before gingerly returning LJ to the stroller and strapping him in. He stirred from his nap and fussed loudly, drawing more eyes to their table.

"Go ahead out to the car, I'll be right there."

Dom handed Layla the keys and she left as quickly as she could through the packed restaurant. When she got to his car, she took Lucas out of the stroller and tried to soothe him a little. But he was woken up from his nap and just wasn't having any of it.

"Sorry, it was like trying to make my way through the jungle there."

Dominique jogged over to the car and Layla handed him his keys. As soon as LJ saw him, his cries quieted some. They all got into the car and Dominique drove back to Layla's soon to be old apartment. Tony was still there, having breakfast.

"Hey Tony, guess what?" Layla said as she stepped into the kitchen.

"What?" He glanced at Dom holding LJ who didn't want to be held by anyone for the time being.

"You all are leaving this place," Dominique said, and Tony's eyes widened in tame surprise.

Layla knew he had to have guessed that was coming. Dominique explained to Tony what he and Layla agreed on. Then it was a matter of putting LJ to sleep while they all pitched in to pack. It didn't take long, because there wasn't much to pack. Mostly they just took their clothes and the essentials for LJ since Dominique wanted to get him new everything. Layla felt as though she were swept up into a storm that was Dominique and knew it wouldn't settle for a while.

Out of all the places Dominique could have put them in, he chose The Langham which was very far away from South Side and very upscale. Layla felt weird simply walking into the ornate lobby next to Dominique. After they packed up he had people clear the apartment out, donating what they didn't need any more and taking the other stuff to be sent ahead to the hotel. She had to say she was amazed at what money could do and how swiftly it got things done.

They didn't even have to check in. As soon as they were in the lobby, someone from the front desk came hurrying up to Dominique.

"Mr. Johnson, I'm Jeffrey, we spoke on the phone. I have your room keys here and can show you up to the suites if you don't mind?"

Jeffrey was dressed in hotel uniform and very professional. He smiled welcomingly at Layla and Tony, then only spared a brief smile toward LJ, who was still attached to his dad. They got to an elevator while Jeffrey listed out all the amenities the hotel had to offer and whatnot. Layla hardly heard any of it though she was just so tired. And it wasn't even midday yet.

When they stepped into Layla and LJ's suite, though, her eyes widened. It was gorgeous and the view of the river and the city was amazing. She'd never seen a place so nice in person before. It was like a very large apartment. There was a huge living room which flowed into the also large dining area. The living room alone must have been the size of Layla's old apartment. Past the living room was a short hallway that led to a master bedroom with a huge en-suite bathroom. Then her room connected to LJ's, which actually had a crib and all inside. Had Dominique really set all that up so quickly?

"My goodness is this all real?" Layla asked as she went back out into the living room.

Jeffery and Tony were missing, so it was just Dom with Lucas sitting on the couch.

"Yes, it's real, Layla," he said and gestured to the couch. "Come, sit, relax a little."

She didn't hesitate to follow orders and sat down on the super comfortable white sectional. Her eyes widened when she noted the giant flat screen TV mounted over a big gas fireplace.

"This is really nice…" she said softly, tears pricking her eyes. "Thank you… You have no idea what this means." She got all choked up as she watched LJ play with Dominique's hair.

"I told you already, I'm taking care of you both. There's no need to thank me; it's what a man is supposed to do." He squeezed Layla's hand briefly and she took a deep steadying breath. "And now you can take a nap. I'll take care of Lucas."

"But when he gets hungry…"

"We took his bottles and formula. I'll figure it out or ask Tony," Dom assured her.

"Okay… but if he gets—"

"We'll be *fine*," he promised her and gestured to the bedroom.

Layla got up and slowly walked toward the bedroom. Dom made Lucas wave to her and she waved back and blew a kiss before she went ahead to the bedroom. When she laid down on the huge king-sized bed, she moaned out loud. It was super comfortable and she knew there was no getting up. Her eyes drooped shut and didn't open again.

"Would you relax please? I told you where I was and what I'm dealing with. We'll talk more when I get home…" Dominique sighed deeply and began speaking intently in French. Layla heard him slam the phone down and take several breaths. Footsteps echoed in the hall, nearing her bedroom and she glanced at the double doors as he quietly stepped in.

"Where is LJ?" she asked him.

"Taking a nap… I think I may need one as well." He sighed and actually pulled off his shoes and socks before climbing into bed with her.

"I heard you on the phone…" she said tentatively.

He brushed a strand of hair behind her ear and gazed intently into her eyes.

"I don't want her anymore." His whisper was barely audible and she wasn't sure she even heard him correctly.

He leaned forward and pressed his lips to hers softly, not in a hurry. Her entire body tingled as goose bumps rose across her skin. He pulled her by the waist, settling her almost underneath him as he pressed his body against hers. Her breathing hitched as her heart rate spiked. Dominique's hand swept down to squeeze her ass and she gasped when his lips slid down to the sensitive skin underneath her neck.

*She felt as though she would combust, though they were still clothed, hardly doing much. Her breathing had turned to swift pants and he held her even tighter against him.*

*"What I love about this most… you're so responsive," he whispered against her skin…*

"Layla…?"

She let out a small gasp as her eyes flew open. Dominique's hand was on her shoulder and he was crouched over her in concern. LJ was whimpering in his arms and reaching for her on the bed.

"Were you having a bad dream?"

She blinked at him in surprise…the dream was so vivid; she swore it was real.

"Uh, yeah… but it was nothing," she murmured while she sat up to take Lucas.

She was glad Dominique woke her up though, before her subconscious could torture her anymore. She couldn't have those feelings for him anymore; he was engaged.

"What time is it?" she asked him and he checked his expensive-looking watch.

"Almost three in the afternoon." He sat down at the edge of the bed and Layla cursed. She had forgotten all about work.

"Crap, I have to call work," she said and glanced around for her bag, remembering that she left it in the living room.

67

"Where do you work?" he asked, standing up with her.

"A diner…" she mumbled before retrieving her phone and calling Jackson.

"Running late, or not coming at all?" he answered.

"I don't think I'll make it in today, can someone cover me?" she asked, feeling horrible. She'd never missed work before, ever. Not counting when she gave birth, of course.

"Yeah, of course. Is LJ doing okay?" he asked.

"He's fine, we just, ah… had a busy morning and I lost track of time," she said.

"Okay then, well, I'll let Macey know to cover for you. Will you make it in tomorrow?" he asked.

"Ah… yeah, I should make it for my shift," she said, hoping that she'd truly be able to.

"All right then, see you tomorrow." Jackson ended the call and Layla wondered where Tony was, then remembered that he actually had work as well.

"Is everything okay with your job?" Dominique asked.

"Yeah, it's fine. I just hardly miss days unexpectedly is all." She shrugged slightly and sat down with LJ. "Are you missing practice today?" she asked him.

"Yeah… but I explained to coach what's going on. He isn't too hard on me about it."

Layla wondered about her dream and if Dominique had actually spoken to his fiancée on the phone or not. "You know we can hire a babysitter for while you're at work. You can interview them yourself if you want," he suggested.

"I don't know how I feel about a babysitter—he's only ever been with family," she said while rubbing LJ's back. Usually he'd be up playing around that time of day, but she knew he was tired.

"That's why we interview them, so we can hire someone we trust. Plus, we'll have to get someone before Tony moves to Maryland..." he pointed out.

"Okay then..." she sighed and peeked down at Lucas who was asleep, his thumb in his mouth and all. "I'm gonna put him down and then shower," she said.

"I'm going to go change and whatnot as well. I'll bring back lunch," he said and got up when she did.

He leaned toward her and she almost held her breath, but then realized he was only kissing Lucas on the head. After that he simply gave her a smile goodbye then he was gone. Layla sighed and went to put Lucas down. She showered and washed her hair, then put something a little nicer on, though she was sure that if she went to explore, the hotel people would notice she didn't really belong.

She had just settled into the living room about to watch TV when Dominique got back.

"Wow, that was fast," she said and he smirked.

"I live close by. I hope you don't mind deep dish?" he asked as he set down two boxes of pizza.

"Not at all, thanks." Layla smiled at him as he sat with her in the living room.

"So when would be a good time for you to interview babysitters? I'm usually free in the mornings or late afternoon…"

"Morning is better." She reached for one of the paper plates he brought with him and served herself some pizza.

"So tomorrow then. And, uh, is it okay if I bring Elle by for dinner tomorrow night?" he asked tentatively.

"Um… she wants to meet me?" Layla asked him with wide eyes.

"Of course! And she'd like to meet Lucas, but only if you're okay with it. If you're ready for that."

"Uh… well, I don't think I'll ever really be *ready* for something like that. But, sure, yeah, you can bring her tomorrow." Layla felt a knot forming in her stomach as she spoke and glanced down at the pizza she once looked forward to eating.

"Is she nice?" Layla couldn't help but asking.

"Yes she's nice, but you have to understand this is… people in our lives will have to get used to this new situation."

"Okay…" Layla put her pizza down and Dominique shook his head, pointing to it.

"Eat something, Layla," he chastised her and she almost rolled her eyes at him.

"You can't expect me to eat right now. I'm too nervous. I'm about to meet *Isabelle* for Pete's sake! I have, like, two of her albums and... I mean, hell, I had a child with her fiancé!"

Dominique chuckled, then he started to laugh. He laughed so hard that tears sprang to his eyes and all Layla could do was stare at him with wide eyes.

"I don't think this is a laughing matter," she said stubbornly.

"It's not, but please just try to imagine she's a normal person at least," he said as he wiped his eyes. "It's easier that way."

"Dominique, you don't understand," she said and got up to pace around the living room.

"I'm just a normal person to you right?" he asked her, suddenly serious.

"Sometimes... like when we're out having coffee or pancakes and no one's noticed you, yes. But not when you go all out on expensive hotels and go about buying Lucas a house... especially not when your fiancée is Isabelle," she said truthfully. "Even if you take away the superstar element to this situation, it's still pretty messed up. To have an illegitimate child with someone who's engaged," Layla mumbled.

"I wasn't engaged when we were together," he said, trying to check the frustration in his tone.

"No, but you were basically on a break with Isabelle right?" Layla turned to face Dominique and in that moment, her emotions surpassing her ability to keep them in check. Then Dominique was truly just a normal guy. "I was just something on the side…"

"Don't do that Layla. You're not just some… 'baby mama,'" he said harshly.

"That's how she'll see me, even worse that I have no money compared to you and you're doing all of… this." Layla shrugged as she glanced in the direction of Lucas's room. "Even if I could imagine you or her as a 'regular' person, whatever that is, this is all still very stressful."

"All right… Okay, I understand. But I need *you* to understand that no one is going to jump down your throat, no one's going to threaten you or hurt Lucas. Not on my watch," he promised her. "So please, just don't worry too much. And don't you worry about what anyone might think or say about my taking care of you and my son. My mind won't change on that."

He gestured to Layla's slice of pizza, she held his gaze for a few seconds before going over to pick up the pizza and sit back down next to him. She knew he was asking her to put some faith in him, but that was hard to just do.

"The pizza is good…" she said and he simply bobbed his head in a nod.

He grabbed the TV remote to put something on to fill the silence. They ate in silence while watching a Lord of the Rings marathon on TBS. Layla couldn't be happier when Tony knocked on the door, she gave him a huge hug when he came inside.

"Miss me?" he chuckled and she nodded vigorously.

"Please, don't leave," she whispered and he laughed again.

"Hey, Tony, how's it going?" Dominique greeted him from the couch with a cool guy handshake.

"Pretty good, have to thank you again for this, man…"

Dominique waved off Tony's thanks and gestured for him to join them on the couch. Layla heard LJ start to cry and she went to go get him for a bath and dinner.

"Wait, wait, you have to teach me all of this."

Dominique caught up with Layla and she had to put away her emotions toward him to put on a smile for Lucas. He stopped his crying and lit up with a big dimpled smile when he saw his mom and dad. Layla instructed Dominique to draw his bath in his little baby tub. Then she showed him how to get him undressed and take care of a dirty diaper if need be. LJ was more vocal and giggly during bath time since he had so much attention. Once he was clean and dressed in his pajamas, LJ looked to Layla for dinner. She let Dominique feed him a bottle though, since he was adamant about learning everything to do with the baby.

73

"He isn't too comfortable with me yet…" Dom noted as he fed LJ, whose eyes were glued to Layla and he complained every time she was out of sight.

"There's just a lot of things changing lately so he's trying to find constants…" she said.

"Oh…" Dominique said quietly.

Layla went into the living room. Tony was texting on his phone, his expression intent.

"What's up?" He looked up at her as she neared him and sighed heavily.

"They need me in Maryland sooner than next week. Want to get me a flight for tomorrow night…" he said and Layla's heart sank.

She was hoping for Tony's support for when she met Isabelle.

"Oh… so soon, though?" she asked him.

"Yeah, I mean, I told them I was already packed up and ready… I just don't want to let this opportunity slip by. This company gives opportunity to move up and this is my next step you know?" Layla sighed and nodded her head.

"Yeah, I know, you have to do what you have to do," she said.

"I know Dom will take care of you guys when I'm gone…"

74

Half of Layla wanted to cry and half of her wanted to ask Tony to stay, but she knew she shouldn't do either or else he would. He was finally doing well and she couldn't weigh him down, especially when she could help it. She saw the water fill up in Tony's eyes and all she could do was hug him.

"I'm so proud of you and I know Ma and Aunt Tae are, too," Layla whispered in his ear.

"I, uh… I have to go pack and uh… I'll stop by tomorrow," he said when she let him go. He stood up and quickly made an exit. Tony never liked to show his emotion.

"What happened?" Dominique asked in a soft curious tone.

"He's leaving tomorrow night… They need him sooner in Maryland," Layla said shakily. She took a deep breath and scrubbed her hands across her face.

"You can always visit. I know LJ will miss his uncle," he said, trying to make her feel better when all she felt was overwhelmed.

"We'll have to find that baby sitter faster than we thought," she said almost numbly.

"It won't be so bad, you know, when you and Lucas are settled in a house and you both get used to everything…"

"I hope not…" she sighed and glanced at the time. It was only seven-thirty. She wondered how long Dominique would stay over, though she wouldn't very well tell him to leave the hotel room he's paying for. Or to say goodnight to Lucas before he was ready. "Oh I have to go call in to work… tomorrow…" Layla realized and she quickly grabbed her phone.

She spoke to Jackson and had to give him a condensed and generic version of what was going on with the move and having Lucas' dad around. Surprisingly, he didn't give her any heat about it and told her to take the time she needed.

"So how'd your job take it?" Dominique asked her. He had put Lucas down to play after burping him. He had some new toys, too, a little basketball he was trying to fit into his mouth and a couple other plush toys.

"Fine, my boss told me to take all the time I needed," she said warily, wondering if Jackson was so nonchalant because his dad was actually selling the diner and they were transitioning or something.

"You look worried."

She shrugged and pushed her hair out of her face. "No, I'm fine. So you actually got him a basketball toy," she said with a small smile as LJ laid on his back happily kicking his legs and still trying to eat the toy ball almost as big as his head.

"Yep and he likes it the best. Like father, like son." Dom smiled happily at LJ as he sat on the blanket with him.

"So will you have a long practice tomorrow since you missed today?" Layla asked him.

"Yeah, I have to go in early, do extra drills. But you know, you and LJ are welcome to watch practice if you want. A lot of the players' families pop in or stay the day. I can get you and LJ clearance." As he spoke, he slid his phone out of his pocket and texted away.

"When do you plan to enroll in physical therapy school?" he asked Layla after he was done doing whatever it was on the phone.

"Well, I have enough money to start in the summer or fall. But before Tony got his job, I was thinking of getting a better job that gets more money before I started school. Just so I don't fall behind with anything."

"You know now that any money you make is yours. LJ's all taken care of so you can get started on your career."

He gave her an encouraging smile and she took a deep breath. She was slowly realizing that indeed Dominique wasn't kidding about being in LJ's life and she *could* finally get her college education.

"Plus, when I find a house for you two, it won't be anywhere near the South Side, if you want to work, you can go ahead and find that better job," he added.

"If I want to work?" she asked slowly.

"You don't have to. If you'd allow it, I'd pay for your school, so you have less to worry about other than LJ and getting your degree," he said in all seriousness, and she knew that all she had to do was say yes and she'd have the scholarship of a lifetime.

But something deep-rooted inside of her wouldn't let her. Maybe it was her upbringing or some pride. She wouldn't take any more handouts from Dominique, not when she had the ability and wellbeing to do things on her own.

"No, I think I should continue doing what I planned, putting myself through school. It'll mean more," she said softly.

"You're a…"

She glanced down at him as he hesitated for a moment, some emotion crossing his features.

"You're a strong person, Layla." Dominique's tone was respectful and for some reason that made Layla's chest constrict and feel warm all at the same time.

"Thank you…"

He simply nodded.

"Do you want to go downstairs for dinner? Or we can call something up?"

"Ah… I'd like to stretch my legs a little," she said and Dominique quickly got up. "Oh, actually, maybe we should call something up instead, he has to be put to bed soon," Layla amended.

To complement her words Lucas let out a perfectly-timed yawn. She picked him up from the floor before Dom could get him.

She felt like he'd been hogging LJ all day, which he had every right to hog him for a while, but still, Layla particularly loved her time rocking Lucas to sleep for the night.

"I guess I'll call room service then. Anything you want in particular?" Dom asked her.

"No, whatever you get will be fine," she said softly as she kissed LJ's soft curls and hugged him to her chest. He snuggled into her warmth and she could hear him sucking on his thumb as she walked back to his room. Layla walked over to the view of the river and sang LJ the lullaby song her mom had sung to her even up until Layla was in high school. It was an old southern hymn about dreaming of starry nights and hopeful whispers from the moon that the sun would be rising soon.

Once LJ was asleep she gingerly laid him in his bed and turned to leave. Only she had to clamp a hand over her mouth to stifle a startled yelp. Dominique was just standing there in the doorway.

"Sorry…" he said with a smirk and she rolled her eyes at him.

"You know, you're kind of scary in the dark; you're like a giant," she said and he snickered.

"You have a beautiful voice," he commented as she left the room and kept the door cracked.

"Thanks, I try to hold a tune for him," she said with a soft chuckle.

"He's lucky. I remember my mother was a horrible singer. She told me that when I was four I asked her to stop singing me to bed and to simply read me a story." He laughed.

"My mom always sang me to sleep. She sang to Tony, too."

"Your mother… where is she?" he asked.

"She died of cancer when I was seventeen. Tony's mom, her sister, died of cancer, too, but when we were much younger."

Dominique's eyes widened and he seemed frankly horrified at what she told him.

"You've been on your own since you were seventeen?"

"Well, I always had Tony," she said slowly.

"Did you finish high school? Do you know your father…?"

Layla didn't understand why Dominique seemed so upset, especially about a past that didn't affect him.

"I got my GED eventually, and no. I never knew him, my mother never told him about me."

"Why not? And what about the cancer, can you or Tony get sick eventually?"

"When my mom first got diagnosed, the hospital that took care of her pulled some strings to get Tony and I genetically tested.

We have a less likely chance. It seemed it only affected our mothers…"

Layla was happy to skirt the topic of her father for the cancer subject, though she didn't want to tell Dominique that even though it was less likely she and Tony would get cancer, they were still more prone to it than others.

"How come your mother never told your father about you?" Dominique asked her again. His eyebrows pulled together and his green eyes darker than she'd ever seen them.

"She felt she could raise me on her own. Without his help… that's all I ever got from her. She never talked about him much. I don't even know his name." Layla sighed with a shrug. "Can we not talk about this stuff anymore?" she asked and rubbed the spot on her chest over her heart.

"Okay, I'm sorry. I just… I can't believe things like this really happen in life. Not just in TV dramas," he said morosely. "I'm sorry you had to grow up like that…" he said with real emotion weighing his tone.

Layla took a deep breath and nodded to herself.

"Yeah, I'm sorry too. But what can you do about the past and circumstance…" She shrugged again and then glanced at the clock near the television. "I'm going to go talk to Tony for a few minutes, come get me when the food is here?"

Dominique nodded and Layla left to walk to Tony's room. He answered as soon as she knocked and met her with a tight hug.

"It's harder than I thought to actually be going..." he sighed, her arm around his waist still, after their hug.

"We've been together all our lives. It's hard for me too," Layla said.

When they stepped into Tony's living room, she saw his suitcases were open and a few piles of folded clothes were still on the floor and couch.

"I'm really gonna miss LJ." He sighed.

They sat down around his bags and Layla occupied her hands by unfolding, then refolding his clothes to put them in the suitcases.

"He's going to miss you too, but I'm really proud of you and I know you'll only continue to move up."

"Promise you'll get a better phone and do the FaceTime or Skype thing with me? And also, I'll try to save up every now and again so you both can visit," he said in all seriousness.

"Don't worry about that; of course we're going to visit each other. And I'll think about the phone thing," Layla said which made Tony chuckle.

"I know Dom will take care of you guys. He's a good man," Tony said while putting some shoes into one of his bags.

"He is, which I find surprising, then half of me is surprised that I'm surprised," she admitted.

"You have to tell me how meeting Isabelle goes. That's got to be bananas."

"I'd actually rather not meet her, but I really have no choice. Dominique wants to be an active part of LJ's life and he comes with a fiancée. So… gonna have to deal with that," Layla sighed.

"It might not be as bad as you think, she could be really nice," he said with a shrug.

"Hopefully. I don't want her hating me and possibly driving Dominique away from LJ."

"Nah, have you seen that guy when it comes to Lucas? It was love at first sight," Tony assured her and she smiled at him.

"What am I going to do without you always in the other room?"

"Call me, anytime," he said and hugged her tight. "I'll always have your back."

# *Chapter 4*

Waking up the next morning to go check on Lucas, Layla was surprised to find Dominique asleep in his room too. He was stretched out on the bed while LJ was still sound asleep in his crib. Dominique's phone was flashing nonstop on the floor and when she peeked over she saw one of his coaches was calling him.

"Dom...?" She gently shook his shoulder and his eyes fluttered open after she gave him another shake. "I think you're late for work," she whispered.

His eyes widened and he practically jumped out of bed and made a grab for his phone.

"*Merde.*"

Layla knew the French word was a curse as she's heard it before on TV. Dominique sat up slowly and rubbed his eyes before he scooped up his phone and sighed as he went through his missed calls and messages.

"I have to go, but if you want to stop by the stadium or go out at all there's a car service at your disposal, just talk to the concierge. It's paid for. But call me if you decide to come to the stadium so I can walk you in," he said quickly.

He went to Lucas's crib and gave LJ a kiss on the head before he waved to Layla and was out the door.

Layla took a breath after the Dominique whirlwind settled and she peeked at LJ who was then wide awake.

"Hey, little man, want to go do some exploring?"

He smiled at her as she picked him up and went out to the kitchenette to make some coffee for herself and mix formula for Lucas. He was talking up a storm as they did their usual morning routine. Only when Layla was about ready to leave the hotel room did she notice a brand new, fancy-looking stroller sitting by the door.

"How does he do it?" she wondered out loud and LJ actually answered back happily and gave her an open mouthed kiss on the cheek. Laughing, she strapped him into the stroller and made sure she had her room key before heading out. "Should we visit the restaurant downstairs, or go outside to walk around…?" Layla figured it was getting too cold to have nice walks out in the city, so she chose to visit the restaurant. Once she exited the elevator to the lobby she found the hotel map and made her way to the restaurant, once she knew where it was.

It wasn't too early in the morning or too close to afternoon so the restaurant was fairly quiet when she walked in.

"Hello, ma'am, welcome to Travelle. Will it just be the two of you this morning?" The kind host gave Layla and Lucas a welcoming smile and she had to say the personnel at Langham were pretty top notch.

"Yes, it's just the two of us," she said and he offered her a seat with a view of the river or a booth seat. She, of course, chose the view of the river. The waiter was right behind the host who explained to her their menu and such. When the waiter left to give Layla time to look things over, she glanced at Lucas, whose wide eyes were riveted on the water and tall buildings.

"This place is really nice, isn't it?" she said and he turned to give her a wide, bubbly smile. She giggled and reached over to wipe his mouth with his bib; even all drooly, Lucas was the cutest baby on Earth. Right after Layla gave her order to the waiter, Tony called her cell.

"Hey, I got off early, they don't want me missing my flight tonight or whatever. Where are you?" he asked when she answered the phone.

"I'm at the restaurant downstairs with Lucas. Wait, they really let you out because they don't want you missing your flight that doesn't take off for another eight hours?"

Tony laughed. "Yeah exactly, but it's cool. I didn't have much to do at work anyway since they know I'm being transferred. I'll meet you at the restaurant in a couple of minutes though," he said and they ended the call.

Layla glanced at Lucas, wondering how she was going to break the news to him. Only a couple minutes later, was Tony shown to Layla's table and LJ was very happy to see his uncle.

"I'm going to miss you *so* much little man," he said and gave Lucas a big kiss on the cheek.

"He's going to miss you, too," Layla said and brushed some of LJ's curls back.

It was really nice to have time with LJ and Tony, talking about everything and having breakfast. When they were done, and ready to leave Layla expected a check, but the waiter told her that everything had been taken care of already. She knew more of Dominique's magic was at work.

"So Dom said I have this car service at my disposal. Before you have to get to the airport, where do you want to go?" she asked.

Tony decided to take a short walk outside. LJ was protected from most of the brisk wind since his stroller kept him largely enclosed.

"Huh... oh, I know! Let's go to the John Hancock Center. See the view from way up," he said eagerly.

"Okay..." Layla said warily.

She really didn't like heights and she was pretty sure Tony knew it. He simply chuckled at her trepidation and she stuck her tongue out at him.

"You have to be strong for LJ or he'll pick up on your mood and get scared when we get up there."

Layla rolled her eyes at him and he chuckled again. "Come on let's go to concierge, they'll hook us up with the ride," she said.

Soon enough, they were on the way in a very fancy Mercedes to one of the tallest buildings in Chicago. It was pretty crowded of course; the building was really famous. There was a wait for them to get out onto the viewing deck and Layla was trying to act like she was having as much fun as Tony was for Lucas's sake. His wide eyes kept landing on her and she knew he was trying to decide if he liked being up so high with so many windows showing the sky.

"How you feeling?" Tony asked her and she gave him a weak smile.

"Not nauseous at all…" she said with a thin smile and, of course, he laughed at her.

"Oh look, it's almost our turn," he said with a wide grin, pointing out at the balcony.

"I think you're going to have to go out there without me…" she said slowly.

"Nope, you have to come out there with us; it's my last wish before I leave." Tony pouted and she sighed heavily, but went outside when the next group was let out.

Layla stayed far away from the edge and refused when Tony wanted to take Lucas out to the edge. It was a tense time, but she faced some of her fear of heights and soon it was over. They were headed back to the hotel around two in the afternoon, LJ needed to eat and hopefully nap.

"So are you ready to fly in a plane?" Layla asked Tony and he nodded, some excitement in his eyes.

"I've never flown before, but people at work say it's awesome, especially if I have a window seat. Which I think I do," he said.

"Then when you get to Maryland?"

"I'm checking into a hotel until I sign the paperwork for my apartment and getting to work. Don't worry—I'll keep you posted every step of the way," he promised.

"Will you come back for Thanksgiving?" she asked him curiously.

"Probably not, but for Christmas, definitely," he promised.

They got back to the hotel and Tony spent time with Lucas before it got time for him to head to the airport. He wouldn't let Layla ride with him so they had a tearful goodbye outside of the hotel. It was almost six when she got back upstairs with Lucas. He finally decided to take his nap and Layla had free time on her hands to do… well, nothing but worry about her coming meeting with Dominique's fiancée of course. What was she going to do for a full hour and a half to calm herself down? She wished briefly that she had some Prozac or something. She ended up watching a bit of TV before checking on Lucas then going to get ready for dinner. By the time she was changed, LJ was awake and she got him ready just in time to grab Dominique's phone call telling her that he was on the way over.

"Layla...?" she heard Dominique's voice sooner than she expected and poked her head out of LJ's room to see that it was just him there.

"Hey, where's Isabelle?" she asked as she went out with LJ in her arms.

"She's on the way. She got held back by a few things. Did I miss Tony?" he asked, surprising her a bit.

"Yeah, he left a few hours ago," she said, a note of melancholy in her voice.

"So what did you do today?" he asked as he took LJ, who was happy to see his dad.

"We went downstairs for breakfast then to the John Hancock Center. Tony guilted me into going. I hate heights."

"You went out today and didn't see anything?" he asked her, a hint of disbelief in his gaze.

"Yeah, what do you mean I didn't see anything?"

Dominique sighed deeply and gestured for Layla to take a seat. "It's leaked, that I have a son. Good thing is no one knows you both are here...yet."

Layla's eyes widened and she searched for something to say.

"Oh…" was all that came out.

"Do you follow the media and whatnot?" he asked.

"No, I mean… I still have a flip phone," she said and he looked at her with the strangest smile, almost as if he was happy that she owned a flip phone.

"You should get a better phone, you know… to Skype Tony and whatnot," he said with a soft chuckle.

"So what are they saying about you having a baby?" Layla asked him.

"Nothing too drastic yet, but they are speculating about my relationship with Isabelle, which she isn't too fond of," he admitted.

"Oh… great," Layla said with a sigh. "So when is she coming, exactly?"

"She should be here soon," he said. "Then we can order some room service, no need to be seen out… all together."

Layla felt as though she was aging from the amount of stress boiling up in her chest. She was through with all the suspense and ready to get their get together over with already. Dominique simply watched her pace around until his phone rang and she assumed it was Isabelle. He spoke for a few minutes then ended the call before he handed her Lucas.

"She's downstairs. I'll be right back," he said and hurried to go and retrieve Isabelle.

"Guess we're meeting your dad's soon-to-be wife…" Layla sighed.

LJ simply stared at her and smiled, ever the happy baby. Five minutes later though, Dominique was back, followed in by Isabelle. She was like a lot of popular female singers Layla guessed. Svelte figure, tan skin, and a pretty face. She noted Isabelle wasn't wearing any makeup though, her brown hair was pulled into a simple ponytail and she was a lot shorter in person than Layla would have guessed. Dominique quite literally dwarfed her. Though that was part of what made her famous, she was known for having a powerful voice that came out of a small body. As soon as she was in the door, her blue eyes scanned the room until they found Layla holding LJ who was staring at Isabelle curiously as well.

"You must be Layla, and the already famous Lucas," she said in a slightly-welcoming tone, mostly cautious though.

Layla noted the sultry rasp to her voice and she could tell that if Isabelle started to sing right then and there, it would sound just like her on one of her albums. No tuning needed.

"Hi, nice to meet you," Layla said with a small smile, feeling awkward as hell.

She'd kill to have Tony with her there. Isabelle's eyes seemed calculating as she studied both Layla and LJ. But Layla caught the brief glimpse of pain as she looked at Lucas who was so obviously his father's son.

"It's nice to meet you, too, I guess…" she finally said and Layla glanced at Dominique when she heard him release a breath, as if he'd been holding it for a while.

They all stood there a bit awkwardly, until LJ reached a hand out towards Isabelle, curious about her.

"Do you want to hold him?" Layla asked, very hesitant though.

"Oh no… it's okay," she said and Layla tried not to bristle at the way Isabelle sized her up, yet again.

"Well, uh, I'm going to go order something to be brought up," he said, effectively leaving the three of them alone.

"So Dominique told me that you and Lucas were living in rather dire straits?" she probed lightly, though Layla already knew what Isabelle thought of her, just from the intensity of her gaze.

"We didn't have a lot of money… but where we were living *would* seem like dire straits compared to this," Layla said with a tiny chuckle.

She wanted to keep the peace, but she wasn't sure she could really do so with the way Isabelle studied her, almost as if she were something below even the ground she walked on. Lucas felt it, too, because he started complaining when his wide eyes landed on Isabelle and soon he was outright crying.

"What's wrong with him?" she asked.

"He's hungry, most likely," Layla said and bounced LJ gently in her arms as she practically made an escape to get one of his bottles.

"Okay, so I ordered food, it'll soon be on the way."

Dominique glanced at Isabelle who had finally sat down on the couch and over at Layla with a crying LJ. Layla watched out of the corner of her eye as Dominique hesitated, but went to rub LJ's back and try to soothe him a little.

"Don't worry, food is on the way," Dominique said and Layla handed him over so she could properly warm up his bottle.

By the time it was warm enough, Dominique was ready to feed LJ on the couch and Lucas was certainly ready to eat.

"Is he usually a happy baby?" Isabelle asked, her voice slightly strained.

Layla found a tiny bit of comfort in the fact that Isabelle was having a hard time with their situation as well, even though Layla knew Isabelle was probably never going to like her.

"Most of the time, yeah, but if he's late in getting his food then he'll complain," Layla said and Isabelle snorted, her gaze touching on Dominique.

"Sounds like someone I know," she murmured.

Layla handed Dominique LJ's bottle and she sat down on one of the sofa chairs across from the couch. Back to feeling awkward, especially without LJ as a shield.

"So how do you guys plan on handling… things? Once Dom moves you and the baby into a house that is." She sighed and glanced at Dominique before looking at Layla.

"How do we plan on handling what?" Layla asked, looking for clarification. Isabelle gave her a bland look for a moment, as if Layla were stupid, before she answered.

"Like, how often will the baby be with you, how often with Dom…? Do you *plan* on, like, being active with Dom's family and whatnot?"

Dominique gave her a warning glance, which she ignored.

"Well, we haven't talked about that yet," Layla said, stifling her sigh. She glanced at the door and wondered how long it would take that room service to arrive.

"Well, maybe we could hash that out tonight," Isabelle suggested and gave a small shrug of the shoulders as she glanced at Dominique.

"Layla and I will talk about that in due time, Elle," Dom said, briefly pausing his feeding LJ, which had him complaining, two seconds away from a full-on wail.

Room service finally came through with the cart of food and Dominique got up to pass LJ to Layla. He quieted as soon as she held him against her chest. She knew LJ wasn't liking Isabelle, which wasn't a great sign in Layla's book.

Isabelle followed Dominique to the dining room and Layla focused on cheering LJ up some. After he finished his bottle and she burped him, he wouldn't settle for anything but being in her arms, so she had to hold him while at the table. Dominique had ordered skirt steak and a variety of sides. Layla put some rice and asparagus on her plate and noted how Isabelle only put veggies and a small piece of meat on her plate.

"Do you think he's missing Tony?" Dom asked, trying to make conversation at the quiet table.

"Probably, yeah. Evenings is usually when he spends time with him," Layla said.

"Who's Tony?" Isabelle asked.

"My cousin. He moved to Maryland for work today. He's been around ever since LJ was born," Layla explained.

"So he was Lucas' father figure then?" she asked innocently enough, and Layla nodded.

"Yeah, I guess so."

She pursed her lips and then glanced down at her plate of food. Her appetite leaving her yet again. She wondered when she'd be able to eat and think normally again, not with her stomach and chest knotted up so tightly all the time. She tried nibbling on some asparagus, ready for their poor excuse for a dinner to be over.

"So, uh… I suppose we'll get going?" Dominique said after a long stretch of painful silence.

Layla looked up in relief and stood up when they did.

"Okay then, we'll, um, see you tomorrow?" Layla asked and he nodded.

"Yeah, I have the day off, so I planned for us to interview nannies," he said. "Then look at some houses I narrowed down," he said.

Layla nodded and noted Isabelle rolling her eyes, thinking no one saw. Dominique definitely didn't.

"Okay then. And, uh, it was nice to meet you, Isabelle," Layla said politely.

Isabelle simply gave her a barely genuine smile before leading Dominique out of the room. When the door closed, Layla let go of a huge breath. LJ looked up at her with wide eyes and she sighed.

"Your dad's fiancée is somethin' else…" she mumbled.

LJ started talking up a storm and Layla knew that if he could speak words, he'd have interesting things to say about Isabelle.

Layla managed to eat a proper dinner once all the tension was leaked from the room and she called housekeeping to retrieve the dinner cart.

She was sitting in the living room with LJ when Tony finally called her.

"How come you didn't call me as soon as you landed?" she answered.

"I had a lot to handle, but I'm finally settled in a little. Only going to be at a hotel for a few days until some things finalize with the apartment. Then I start training tomorrow. It's a lot," he sighed, but Layla heard that he was excited about it all in his voice. "So how was meeting Isabelle? Wait, am I interrupting?"

"No, you're not interrupting. They left early because the whole thing was so awkward. It's obvious she doesn't like me and hasn't gotten used to the fact that Dom has a son at all. Here I was freaking out, I actually feel more sorry for *her*," Layla said. She played with one of Lucas' new dragon plush toys and he laughed when she wiggled it at him and tickled his neck.

"Damn, that's... that sucks balls," he said, making Layla laugh.

"It *does*. I just don't know how it's going to work with her. Especially when Dom and I haven't even figured out all the details yet."

"What details?"

"Like when will LJ spend time with him, how much time, will I be a part of Dominique's family or not. That sort of thing," she sighed.

"Do you want to be a part of his family?" Tony asked her.

"Well, I want to know the people Lucas will be around, so I guess that's a yes. But then that's..." Layla paused to shake her head back and forth. "I just know she and I will clash often. Especially when they get married and start having kids of their own," she said.

"What if he leaves her for you?" Tony said, playing devil's advocate.

"Stop, don't even put that in my head. I already had a... weird dream about Dominique," she said and Tony laughed.

"I think a lot of women have had 'weird' dreams about him. Plus, you have more to go on. You made LJ didn't you?"

Layla couldn't help but laugh.

"Shut up, Lucas happened to be immaculate conception...via borrowing Dominique's genes," she joked, cracking Tony up into laughter.

"Right, 'borrowing,'" he chuckled.

"Anyhow, I think Lucas and I are in for an interesting holiday season," Layla sighed.

"Yeah, Thanksgiving is right around the corner, but I think Dominique is playing a Thanksgiving game." Tony filled Layla in on The Horns' schedule and she had an idea for when she could expect him to be busy. They didn't have another game until Friday, the day after next.

"All right… I don't want you to be late for work in the morning, I'll let you go. Plus, LJ just fell asleep and his legs are sticking up in the air," she said fondly while smiling at LJ asleep on his play blanket.

"Aw you gotta send me a picture of that." He laughed and Layla promised she would. After ending the call, she quickly got the perfect picture and sent it to both Tony and Dominique. Tony sent back a bunch of hearts and a teary face, Dominique texted her back that he was coming over. Her heart did a small stutter as she wondered why he was coming back for another night… but maybe he wanted to sleep next to LJ again. She picked Lucas up and took him to his crib. She definitely envied him his happy oblivion. What she'd give to sleep as peacefully as he was.

Layla waited up for Dominique; he came about an hour later, around ten, wearing sweat pants and a sweat shirt.

"You didn't have to wait up for me," he said and went over to sit heavily on the couch with a troubled sigh.

"She doesn't like me, does she?"

Dominique snorted, then chuckled without humor.

"You were right—this is a messed up situation. Not everyone can fall in love with LJ like I did I guess." He sighed.

"I don't know, maybe Isabelle is just used to cute babies or something, I'm pretty sure LJ has powers."

"Is he asleep?" he asked and Layla nodded.

100

"Yeah, you can go in there if you want," she said.

"In a little bit, but I think we should talk…" he said slowly. She simply looked at him expectantly and held her breath. "Like about what Elle was asking?"

"Do you want me meeting your family? I mean… I'd like to know who LJ's going to be around, you know?"

"Of course, of course I have no problem with you meeting them. In fact, I *want* you to meet them. But about the time I spend with him. Do we go half and half? What are you comfortable with?"

"Uh… well… what do you mean by 'half and half'?" she asked, sort of horrified at the prospect of spending even a night away from LJ. Her palms were even sweating.

"Maybe one week with me, one week with you…?" Layla was shaking her head before he finished speaking.

"I get heart palpitations just thinking about that…" she admitted.

"Well of course it's going to be hard the first few times… but soon you'll be starting school and I'm sure you'll need some time off from him."

Layla took a deep breath and rubbed her temples.

"Can we not talk about that right now? I mean he's not even six months yet," she said anxiously.

"This isn't ideal for either of us," he said.

"I don't know… I just… I don't know." Layla didn't know she'd feel so anxious talking about simple custody issues.

"All right, when he's not so dependent on breast feeding then? Six months, we'll talk about it again?"

Layla nodded, the constricting in her chest only easing a little.

"I keep underestimating how hard this is going to be," she said and stood up to pace around.

"Just forget about it for now. Get to know me better, my family. Then we can talk about what time he'll spend with me. Hell, when he turns six months I'll be happy with weekends even." The tension in her chest dissipated some more and she nodded.

"Okay, that sounds better," she said softly.

"I got you something… and I'm going to urge you not to fight me on this. Please." He reached down and pulled a bag that was hiding on the floor, near the couch's arm rest.

"You came in with that?" she asked, studying the white plastic bag until she saw the Verizon logo on it. "Dominique you did *not* get me a phone!" she said, upset. "You don't have to get me things," she said adamantly.

"You have a flip phone, Layla, please just take it. I have an extra line on my plan anyway. What if I want to Skype with LJ?" he asked her.

She took several deep breaths and simply stared at him disapprovingly with her hands on her hips.

"You shouldn't have gotten that," she said as he pulled out the box with the cell phone in it.

"You're going to have a new number, too, so make sure to call Tony and whoever else."

Layla simply continued to stare at him disapprovingly. He set the box down on the couch and stood up, slowly walking toward her. His eyes were intent on hers and a bright green, never moving from her gaze. She stopped breathing when he got close enough that she smelled the clean scent of soap and shampoo on him. She had such an urge to close her eyes and lean into him. He simply reached behind her, slid his hand into her back pocket, and stole her phone before she could grab it from his hand.

"Hey!"

He grinned boyishly and quickly plopped back onto the couch. "Don't worry; I'll set this up for you and teach you how to use it." He grinned.

"Fine… What is it?" she asked and moved closer to look at the box.

"A Samsung Galaxy S7 Edge. You'll like it once you get used to it." He smiled at her meaningfully and she rolled her eyes at him, which only made him chuckle.

"Why does it have to have so many names? And what does the seven mean?" she asked and Dominique stared at her with a dropped jaw.

"Don't you watch TV? Go on the internet?" he asked her in shock.

"No. I only had Netflix and didn't have a computer," she said.

Dominique groaned, closing his eyes briefly.

"This makes me want to… it's like you haven't…" He sighed heavily and simply shook his head before focusing on the phone once more.

Layla sat down next to him to watch what he was doing with the phone. It took Dominique about two hours to teach her the basics of having a smart phone.

"There's so much about you having a baby on Twitter," Layla said as she scrolled through the search results on Google. She was curious about what people were saying.

"Yeah, Twitter is a black hole…" he mumbled.

"Why don't you post a picture of him?" Layla suggested.

"I'd rather keep things as private as possible for as long as I can. If I post a picture of Lucas, making him legitimately real, the media will be all over us."

"Oh, I see…" she said and exited Chrome to text the few contacts she had that she had gotten a new number.

"We're going to have a full day tomorrow." Dominique yawned and stretched.

That reminded Layla that she needed to use her breast pump.

"Are you staying over?" she asked him and he nodded slowly.

"Is that all right?"

"Of course, I was just wondering. I have to, um, do something is all," she said awkwardly.

"What is it?" he asked curiously.

"I have to use the… well, LJ has no more bottled breast milk and he usually likes that better than formula," she explained and it took only a moment before Dominique understood.

"Oh, okay then," he said slowly.

"I'll just do it in the room."

Layla wished she wasn't so awkward, but all the words were already out there. She shook her head to herself as she got up and tiptoed into LJ's room to retrieve the breast pump. She spent forever in her room filling up a couple of bottles then stashed them in the fridge. She was surprised to see Dominique still out on the couch intently on his phone.

"I won't turn into one of those cell phone zombies now, will I?" she asked him, only half-joking.

"No, no… I'm just texting Isabelle. We had an argument. Have been arguing since I told her about LJ." He sighed.

"I'm sorry," Layla said sincerely, she liked seeing Dominique happy and joking, not so bummed out.

"Does the breast pump hurt?" he asked her, abruptly changing the subject.

"Ah, yes, actually it does. I'd much rather breast feed, but I always feel weird pulling out my boob in case we're out," she admitted. "I know many moms simply throw a blanket over their shoulders for privacy and go about their lives, but I guess I'm shy." She shrugged.

"You are shy. You were at that game where we met."

He gave her a small smile and she remembered how Dominique had to constantly tell her to stay until after the game. She couldn't believe he was actually talking to her until he legitimately walked up to her to properly introduce himself.

"You told me that I seemed like a normal person." She chuckled and he laughed.

"I have to admit that even with all of the gifts God gave me, talking to women I'm interested in isn't one of them." He chuckled. Layla smiled, followed by a huge yawn and they snapped out of their little moment down memory lane.

"It's late…" he said and she stood up when he did. They said their goodnight and went to sleep in separate rooms. Layla prayed that she wouldn't dream of him again and instead have a dreamless sleep. But of course her night was filled with tossing and turning and Dominique's blazing green eyes.

She hardly got a full three hours sleep before she felt baby hands on her face and a wet kiss on her cheek.

"Say, 'mama wake up.'" Dominique tried to put on a baby voice and that definitely put a smile on her face along with LJ's good morning kisses. She opened her eyes and saw that Dominique looked pretty tired.

"Didn't get much sleep either?" she asked.

"Either? Thought Lucas and I were the only ones," he smirked. "LJ didn't want to sleep very much."

"Oh… seriously?"

"Yep, we stayed up talking for most of the night, until he fell asleep again," he explained.

"Well, welcome to parenthood," she said and Dominique let out a hearty laugh.

"It makes me wonder how you did it when he was newborn…" he said softly when he sobered.

"I had Tony. If I didn't, I don't know that I'd be sane, to be honest," she said, more truthful with Dom than she intended to be.

He sat down on the bed with her, LJ still basically tasting Layla's cheek. She picked him up and sat up, wiping her face in the process.

"So we have several nannies to interview this morning, then afterwards we're going to choose a house today."

He gave her the schedule for the day and she almost reluctantly got out of bed to shower and change into something nice and presentable. She even put her hair into a slightly-fancy ponytail, just because.

"Wow, you look… really nice," Dominique said when Layla came out. He already had LJ ready and was, himself, looking incredibly GQ in an olive green pullover and well-fitting khaki pants. He was perfectly put together, his hair curling just right around his shoulders and framing his face, his five o'clock shadow perfectly accenting his jaw. Layla, for a second, couldn't believe his looks. Then she came back to Earth and forced herself to be cool.

"Thanks. You look like you," she said, which made him laugh.

"I was thinking, if we get done with things early, we can go shopping for LJ a little bit, get him some clothes and new toys. Oh I almost forgot to tell you, I made the appointment at city hall to put my name on his birth certificate. We have to make an appointment to get a paternity test before going to amend his certificate,"

"Oh... uh, okay then. Well, during the week is best for me, anytime in the morning," she told him and he nodded, making note of it.

"We have time for breakfast if you want."

"Can we go downstairs?" Layla asked.

She really liked that restaurant. Though when Dominique hesitated, she deflated a little.

"We can go, if you really want to," he said, noting her disappointment.

"No, no, if you don't want people to see. It's okay," she said and went to go grab the hotel line to call for room service. But Dominique caught her arm before she could.

"We can go downstairs, Layla, it's fine," he said and she shook her head no.

"No, I don't want to... start anything," she said.

"When we go out later, people are bound to see us. LJ can't stay secret forever," he said and then walked over to LJ's new stroller.

"All right, if you're okay with it," she said.

Layla chewed on her lip absently as she watched Dom strap Lucas in, then he expertly packed his baby bag and slid it onto the stroller.

"You're almost a pro," Layla said and he chuckled.

"I'm a fast learner, plus Lucas is mostly easy going so that helps," he said.

Layla followed Dominique out into the hall and down to the elevator. She remembered the last time she went downstairs everything was pretty normal for a hotel. Everyone was about their business and the staff was politely helpful, but not too in your face. As soon as they stepped out of the elevator and into the marble lobby, the people waiting for the elevator took one look at Dom and got all wide-eyed. It was insane at how much sudden attention he drew.

"You're The Dom! Dominique Johnson, way to go in the last game man!" A kid, probably fourteen or fifteen spoke to Dominique excitedly while his dad poked him not so subtly in the side.

"Thank you." He smiled politely at the kid who was pulling out his phone, definitely wanting a picture. But his dad thankfully pulled him towards the elevator, giving Dom a mumbled apology.

"No, it's all right I can take a picture." Dominique glanced at Layla and she stepped forward to push LJ's stroller. "Go ahead, I'll catch up," he told her and she rolled away towards the restaurant.

"Your dad's famous," she said to LJ who simply gave her a one dimpled smile and stuck his little fist into his mouth. Yep, Lucas had *no* clue what was going on.

# *Chapter5*

Once Dominique finally made it to Travelle, Layla was being served her breakfast already.

"How do you go out?" she asked him, genuinely curious. It seemed he had to be dressed in a hoodie or baseball cap in order to get by relatively unnoticed.

"Usually people can gauge whether or not you want to be bothered, especially if you're not staying in one place for a little while. But kids usually don't care either way, they'll chase you down," he said with a chuckle.

"Oh…" she said and took a bite of her scrambled eggs.

"Yeah, if you can help it, simply be successful without being famous," he advised her before telling the waiting server what he wanted to eat.

"Did you feed him already?" she asked Dominique as she glanced at Lucas, who was staring out of the window at the sky, almost in a trance.

"Yes, one of the breast milk bottles," he said and tickled LJ's chin, snapping him out of whatever train of baby thought he was on. Other than the elevator scene, they managed to have a regular breakfast. Afterwards they made it upstairs just in time to greet the first nanny candidate.

Layla liked the way she looked, she was most likely in her forties, kind brown eyes and a warm smile. Her dark brown hair was pulled up into a ponytail and she wore a simple outfit, a nice sweater and jeans with a pair of fall boots.

"Hello, I'm Nadia, from the nanny service," she greeted them when they reached the door, shaking both Layla's hand and Dominique's. "I was beginning to think that I was too early," she joked.

"Oh, not at all, we were just coming up from breakfast," Layla said.

Dominique opened the door, letting them all in and Nadia bent down to say hi to Lucas in his stroller. He had a huge smile for her and reached out to touch her face.

"Oh, this must be Lucas; he's the cutest thing in this world!" she gushed and Layla smiled.

She definitely thought so herself. She was beginning to think that Nadia might be the nanny for them, no need to interview anyone else.

"So take a seat. Why don't you tell us about yourself and your experience?" Dominique invited her to sit in the living room and she handed them both copies of her references and resume.

"Well, I just left a family that I've been working for, for seven years. Their youngest is seven years old and I've been with her all her life. They recently moved out of state so that is why I could no longer work for them. But I have a lot of experience with children newborn to ten years old…" Nadia went on to talk herself up while Layla and Dominique listened. Even LJ listened while he stared at her from Layla's lap. Everything sounded good to Layla. As far as she was concerned they could hire Nadia right away, she just felt that comfortable with her.

After Nadia left, they saw three more women, all older than Nadia, and a little more brusque. After the flurry of interviewing, Layla got ready to feed LJ his lunch.

"I liked Nadia best, the others seemed too… I don't know, Mrs. Doubtfire meets Supernanny."

Dominique burst into laughter at that and LJ laughed at his dad laughing. "Yeah, Nadia is the best to me, too. An old teammate of mine actually suggested her," he said, still chuckling.

After taking care of LJ and hanging out for a bit they went out to go look at houses, all near Dominique's house on the Near West Side.

"So how many places are we looking at?" she asked him when they were on the way.

"Five. A couple of condos and three townhouses," he said. "We're going to meet the realtor at my house, then all the places are in walking distance."

"That's convenient," Layla said in a low voice and glanced back at LJ.

He was looking out at the city as they drove through it. When they got to Dominique's town house, Layla was still a little dazed at how nice it was every time she went. His driveway wrapped around to a garage at the back of the house and inside was all modern and contemporary, decorated in light colors and high-end finishes.

"Hey, I want to show you something," he said when they all got inside, LJ in Dominique's arms.

"What?" she asked and he took her hand to lead her up to the second floor. They passed his bedroom and he led her into the guest room right next to it. Layla gasped when she walked into a gorgeous nursery. It wasn't your typical blue, or boyish colors. There were vibrant reds, greens, blues, and such to make Lucas's eyes pop with wonder.

"This is his room?" she said as she walked inside and saw a brand new crib, changing table, new toys, and everything LJ needed. Tears came to her eyes then; Lucas would never want for anything. "He's all set," she said, still a little in awe.

"I know he likes it. Look." Dominique chuckled and Layla glanced back to see Lucas talking up a storm and looking at everything.

"It's perfect, Dom," she said and smiled at him.

The doorbell rang downstairs and Layla figured that must be the realtor. They all went downstairs and Dominique let the realtor in, who introduced himself as Zach. After that they went about taking a look at the places Dominique narrowed down for Layla and LJ. After looking at the condos and a couple of the townhomes, there was one left. As soon as they walked up to it, Layla already fell in love with the outside. There was a gate and the outside of the house was warm, clean, and contemporary looking. When they walked into the warm interior, all redone and modern, LJ spoke up, seeming to like the place. Layla liked it, too, with the wooden floors and open floor plan.

"I already love it," she said, which made Dom chuckle.

"Yeah, LJ does, too," he said. "I think it's the best one too…" he added and the realtor showed them the rest of the house. It was technically three stories, with the third floor being a loft library area.

"All right, so if we're certain, we can go ahead and get the paperwork signed and get you this house." After seeing the full house, Zach got things going with the paperwork on the house and Layla felt sort of like her head was spinning.

"Hey, Layla, I think Lucas wants his mom."

Dominique handed the baby to her before they left the townhouse to walk back to Dominique's place. Layla paused when they got to the gate, to put LJ in his stroller. She glanced across the street briefly and thought she saw some guy with a camera pointed at them. But Dominique called her forward and she hurried to catch up with them.

***

"Zach works fast," Layla said as she sat down on Dominique's couch, holding the keys to her and Lucas' new place.

"Yep, all we have to do is get some furniture in there and you're all set." Dominique smiled at her and she gave him one in return.

"I really… I have to thank you for all of this. It's—you've gone above and beyond for us," she said shakily. Strong feelings of gratitude and other emotions threatened to overwhelm her.

"Like I said before Layla, it's what I'm supposed to do. Plus, I love LJ and want the best for him. That means taking care of you both," he said and leaned over to give her a brief kiss on the cheek.

LJ gave a happy baby noise and kissed Dominique on the chin, or rather he simply put his mouth on Dom's chin and left some affectionate drool.

"He gave me a kiss! That's the first time," Dominique said with a laugh as he wiped his chin.

"That means he likes you," Layla said with a smirk.

Dominique's phone started to ring and he fished it out of his pocket while holding LJ up on his lap.

"What? Are you kidding?" Dominique's tone was surprised and angry all of a sudden. Then Layla heard a shrill voice from the other line and Dom held the phone away from his ear in annoyance briefly. "Calm down, relax, I'll send someone for you," he said then ended the call.

"What happened?" Layla asked curiously.

"It's news now that I have LJ, and the paparazzi are all over Elle. Can you stay here until I come back? Don't leave the house." He gave her LJ who complained and reached out for Dominique. "I'll be back," he murmured before kissing Lucas on the head and hurrying out of the family room, keys in hand and phone already back to his ear.

"Guess it's just us then…" Layla sighed.

She got up to put LJ down in his play pen for a moment so that she could peek out of the window. She saw Dominique's car backing out of the drive and she also saw some people waiting by the gate out front. Most of them had cameras and they actually attempted to crowd around his car as it was moving onto the main road. Layla's brows lifted in shock; she didn't realize things like that actually happened to people.

One of the people glanced back at the house and pointed directly at Layla. She closed the drape before he could lift his camera to snap a picture. Her phone started ringing then and she was glad to see Tony calling.

"Hey, you won't believe what I just saw," he said as soon as she answered.

Layla sat and looked at LJ who was pleasantly chewing on one of his toys and staring at her adoringly. She smiled at him, thanking the Lord that she lucked out with such a happy baby.

"You won't believe what's going on here. I mean, you always hear about celebrities dealing with the 'paparazzi,' but it's real. There's a small group of them outside of Dominique's house," she told him, trying to peek outside again without disturbing the drapes.

"I was on break and they have the news channel on in the staff room. You know how they do the little entertainment sections right?"

"Yeah, what'd you see?" she asked him.

"They snapped a picture of you, Dom, and LJ walking out in the city. Confirming that he has a son with someone that's not Isabelle. People are speculating about their relationship, bashing her character a little," he said with a bit of pity in his voice. "You said she was nice when y'all met right?"

"I think she was nice enough just because Dominique was around, and the baby. But I don't know… I know she doesn't like me, that's for sure." Layla sighed.

"Well, be careful, don't let them get a clear picture of you or people will start saying all kinds of things. Especially when they don't know anything," he said.

After catching up a little with Tony, he got Layla to try Skype and he got to see LJ, even though LJ simply wanted to put the phone in his mouth.

"When you move into the new place, Skype me so I can see it, okay?" he said as they were about to end the call.

Layla promised she would and then their call ended. She went about warming up LJ's bottle just as Dominique got back with Isabelle right behind him.

"I just don't like what they're saying about us, about *me*. I'm not like that and it can hurt my fan base…" she stopped talking as soon as she saw Layla at the stove, holding LJ's bottle.

"Hi, Isabelle," Layla said awkwardly.

"Hey, Layla," she said in a swift and bored tone before she sent a sideways glance at Dominique. "I see you guys picked out a house today," she added. Her tone changed, becoming almost polite.

"Yeah, it's right around the corner. LJ got all excited as soon as we walked through the door so he picked it out as much as we did," Layla said with a smile, trying to keep away from any negativity as much as possible.

"That's interesting. I didn't know three-month-olds were aware of much," she said.

"Lucas is smarter than most babies," Dominique said and pulled Isabelle aside to the kitchen island.

Layla went about warming up the bottle. She had left Lucas in his play pen after figuring out how to use the baby monitors Dominique had. The monitor was sitting on the island, and when Layla glanced back at it she heard LJ start complaining for being left alone too long. Isabelle picked the monitor up in annoyance and turned it down, she and Dominique were having some intent conversation.

"I'm sorry, but can you watch this while I go check on him?" she asked Dominique who nodded.

Isabelle glanced at Layla, even more annoyed, before she left to go and pick LJ up from the play pen. He was hungry, of course, so he didn't stop his fussing as she carried him into the kitchen.

"I think it's warm enough for him," Dominique said as Layla entered the kitchen. He handed her the bottle and she tested it before feeding LJ.

"So, I hired some security for you and LJ, just for the time being. To keep the cameras and such away."

Layla paused for a moment, taking that in, while Isabelle sighed.

"This is ridiculous," she murmured and Layla was thinking the same thing.

"Is that necessary?" Layla asked him.

"Yes, they're outside the house as we speak," he said, and she could hear the exasperation in his voice. "How are you going to get back to the hotel? How are you going to get to work without having them herded away?"

"All right, fine, fine. Whatever you think is best," she conceded.

Layla glanced down at LJ who was staring at her with his big green eyes. She felt Isabelle's gaze on her and grew uncomfortable simply standing there in the kitchen with them, so she wandered back into the family room. Layla had enough time to feed LJ, burp him and begin rocking him for a nap by the time Dominique and Isabelle wandered into the family room.

"Is it okay if we watch something? Or will he wake up?" she asked Layla while reaching for the remote.

"I'll go put him down in the crib, it's fine," Layla said. She went with LJ to his new room and made sure he was pretty sound asleep before putting him down in the crib. Afterwards she grabbed the baby monitor to put it in there with him and hesitated before she forced herself to go join Dominique and Isabelle. When she stepped into the family room, they looked quite cuddly on the couch. Layla ignored the pang of... what, jealousy? Hurt? Either way, she refused to acknowledge it and tried to forge ahead in making their situation work for LJ's sake.

"So how is Tony doing? Have you tried to Skype with him yet?" Dom asked Layla as she sat down on the couch, as far from them as she possibly could.

121

"He's good, we talked to him earlier and he told me how to use the Skype thing. So he got to see LJ."

Dominique nodded, with a smile. "That's cool. So is he coming for Thanksgiving…?"

"No, he won't make it that soon," she said and Isabelle glanced up at Dominique briefly, before she studiously looked ahead at the television.

"Well, you should have early dinner with us. I have a game that day, but we usually eat at my dad's. It's more like Thanksgiving brunch." He chuckled.

Layla's eyes widened a bit and she couldn't help but glance at Isabelle who was changing the channels until she stopped on the Entertainment channel. Her face was at the top right of the screen while a woman talked about Isabelle's latest tour.

"People still think I'm in the UK?" she murmured.

Dominique nudged Layla's arm and she glanced at him.

"So will you? I already told the whole family about LJ. My dad definitely wants to meet him." He looked at her with a small playful pout and she nodded.

"Yeah, okay… Sure," she said hesitantly.

Dominique gave her a look of concern and opened his mouth to ask her something, but Isabelle turned his attention to the TV.

"Look, they're saying I'm still in the UK and have no idea what you're 'up to,'" she sighed and Layla saw a photo of Dominique walking next to Zach, his realtor, and then Layla pushing LJ's stroller.

"So how about we go outside now, let them get a photo?" he suggested.

Layla could tell he was mostly teasing, but Isabelle stood up, ready to go.

"That's not a bad idea. Let's go for a stroll," she said, both annoyance and determination in her tone.

"Why can't you just tweet something and make it go away?" Dominique asked.

"Come on, Dominique," she said adamantly.

He sighed, then got up and reluctantly followed her out. Layla could hear the flashes of cameras as soon as they opened the front door. The camera flashes were intermingled with shouts for their attention. Layla couldn't believe Isabelle was that concerned with what the media was saying about her.

Curious, Layla used her phone to do a Google search on Isabelle. She saw very recent articles, all speculating on her relationship with Dominique. It seemed most people thought she had screwed up their relationship yet again and that Dominique was finally done with her. They were painting her as the pining other woman, trying to win his affections back, though the truth was far

123

from that. After her brief research, Layla wondered how she'd make it back to the hotel with LJ.

*"The worst* idea you've ever had," Dominique said angrily as they got back to the house, slamming the door behind them.

Layla checked the time and saw they'd only been out like fifteen minutes. She looked up and realized they were followed in by two guys wearing dark clothing. *Huge* guys wearing dark clothing and following behind Dominique and a pissed looking Isabelle.

"So what? We didn't make it to the ice cream parlor," she said with a shrug and began going off in French which Dominique argued with her in kind.

"So… uh, what happened?" Layla asked, her eyes wide at their heated display.

Meanwhile, the men whom she assumed were security simply stood in the periphery, stoic, but watchful.

"We tried taking a 'walk' like this one suggested and nearly got rundown by the fucking media mob." He gestured outside angrily and Isabelle rolled her eyes.

"You never want to listen to what I have to say. It was a good idea!" she said.

"It wasn't; you know how they are. You're claustrophobic for Christ's sake!"

Layla's eyebrows were touching her hairline then, she felt as if she should excuse herself or something. When she heard LJ start to cry from the monitor she switched gears, her concern for Lucas blocking out all else, and shushed them.

"You two are yelling way too loud," she said with only a little force in her tone.

Shaking her head, she sighed and walked past them to go and try to rock LJ back to sleep. He was really crying, not just complaining, by the time she got to his room. When she picked him up she felt that his temperature was up.

"Is he okay?"

Dominique startled Layla a bit, which only made LJ cry even harder.

"He's just upset," she said.

LJ had only been in such hot displeasure once before. And that was when he was tired *and* hungry.

"She left..." he said sheepishly.

Layla turned around to give him a slight frown.

"You really didn't have to yell at her like that," she said admonishingly. "Do you argue so explosively all the time?"

Layla walked over to the changing table to put LJ into a clean diaper and changed his clothes, putting on a dry undershirt onesie and slipping some socks onto his feet. She turned the fan on low before she took him and sat down on the rocking chair. Dominique was standing like a tall statue by the door, his expression like one of the bodyguards in the family room.

"We do… that's why sometimes I just need a break from her. Things had been finally really great between us. So perfect… she just has the worst time adjusting to things. It tears us apart *every time*," he sighed.

"Well… you've been with her a while. You know her, just let her handle things the only way she knows how."

Layla felt as if she should go into counselling instead of physical therapy.

"You're right, thanks," he said with a small smile. "So, uh… do you want to meet your security?" he asked her, a little sheepish.

"They weren't with Isabelle?" she asked him curiously.

"One of them was, the other had gotten here just in time," he said with a sigh.

Layla looked down at LJ who still seemed upset and was refusing to close his eyes. She bent down to kiss his forehead and brush his hair back.

"Did we scare him?" Dominique asked in a low voice.

Layla could hear the remorse there and glanced up at him briefly.

"Yeah, most likely. He's always been in mostly happy environments," she explained gently, but pointedly.

"I'm sorry, little man, sorry for yelling." He walked over to kiss Lucas on the forehead.

After a few minutes, LJ fell back to sleep and Layla gingerly put him into his crib. She followed Dominique out to meet the security guy. He could have been a football player or something. He had dark caramel colored skin and his black hair was cut low, almost military style. He had very angular features, a straight nose and full lips. He was definitely handsome, but aloof, maybe he'd been a police officer, or in the military before going into security.

"Layla, this is John; he's one of the best." Dominique briefly introduced them and John actually gave Layla a polite smile.

"Nice to meet you, miss." He shook Layla's hand and she gave him a polite smile as well. "You don't have to worry about those camera people out there. They might snap a picture or two, but they won't get close," he assured her.

"So you'll just, I don't know, follow us around?" she asked, really not knowing how else to phrase that question.

"Well, I'll act as your driver and escort you in and out of wherever you go. If you need me to follow you around anywhere beyond that, I will," he said respectfully.

"Okay then, that sounds reasonable," she said with a nod and he inclined his head.

"It would be appropriate if we exchanged numbers, just to make things simpler," he said and she exchanged numbers with him. Afterwards he let her and Dominique know that he'd be outside.

"So… I have a driver…" Layla said with a sigh and Dominique gave her a warning look.

"It's needed, don't protest," he said with an upheld hand.

Layla's phone rang and she wondered if it was John calling, but she saw it was Mr. Joe.

"Hello? Mr. Joe?" she answered.

"Layla, how are you?" he asked with a heavy sigh.

"Oh, I'm fine… is everything okay with the diner?" she asked anxiously.

"Well, I know that Jackson told you some things, some things that are true. I've had to sell to IHOP and it will be a long time before they overhaul the building. By the time they are ready to open, I think it will be best to just find another job instead of waiting so long," he explained.

"Wait… So they will re-hire everyone, it'll just be a while until they do?"

"Yes, exactly." He sighed.

Layla rubbed her temples and stifled her sigh.

"So that's that then, huh?" she said.

"I'm afraid so. I am sorry Layla," he said and she smiled.

Mr. Joe was a good guy even though he had his moments.

"It's all right, Mr. Joe, I understand. Tell Jackson I said good luck with everything," she said, and they ended the call shortly after.

"What happened?" Dominique asked her, his expression concerned.

"It's uh, the diner I work, well, worked at—it closed down, basically." She sighed and ran her fingers through her hair, undoing her ponytail in the process.

"You would have quit anyhow, right?"

"Yeah, I would have, when I had another job in the bag," she murmured and thought back to the last time she job searched. "Guess I just wasn't exactly ready to get back to the job search."

"What about school? Have you applied anywhere yet?"

"I was thinking to do it after everything here gets settled. You know, once the house is ready and whatnot."

"Oh that reminds me, you have to settle on a design for the house, so the decorator can order what's needed," he said and got up.

He told her he'd go get his laptop and be right back. Layla made a plan to get started on a new job and applying to the technical schools in the city once she and LJ were settled in the new house.

"You said the house would be ready in a few days, right?" she asked Dom when he walked back into the room.

As he showed her the several aesthetic designs for furnishing the house, he filled her in on everything. Once LJ was awake from his nap, Layla wanted to head back to the hotel early. It was strange having John drive them and escort her up to the room, but she figured she'd deal with it for the time being.

Having a quiet evening with LJ was much needed, especially after his nap interruption from the afternoon. Oddly enough, after the stress of the day, Layla finally had a full night's sleep.

When she woke the next morning, she went to check on LJ, and was surprised to see Dominique was in LJ's room.

"What are you doing here?" she asked him groggily.

"I couldn't stay away," he admitted with a sheepish chuckle. "I just felt like he might not like me after yesterday," he admitted.

Layla's eyes opened enough for her to see he was dressed in his team sweats, his hair pulled up into a little ponytail.

"On your way to work?"

"Yeah I have practice until six. Do you want to come over for dinner later?" he asked her.

"Sure, we'll come by. And LJ loves you, don't worry about him," she assured Dominique.

He smiled at her warmly and surprised her with a kiss on the cheek after giving one to LJ. As she went to pick up LJ, she wondered what she would do with her day. It was only Monday and she had LJ; it wasn't like she could go out, especially with potential cameras scouting out for she and Lucas.

She did manage to go down for breakfast with LJ without being bothered, though the wait staff that she was getting to know did have a bit more interest in she and Lucas. She minded the attention, but Lucas certainly didn't. She did peg some jobs that she could apply for after doing a light search on her phone and the rest of the day was spent in the suite with LJ up until it was time for her to head over to Dominique's for dinner.

"Ready to go see daddy?" she asked LJ as they waited for John to get to the hotel. Lucas actually gave a little squeal just as John knocked on the door.

"Hi, Layla, ready to go?" John smiled welcomingly at her when she opened the door for him. He bent down to tickle Lucas' chin, making the baby laugh.

"Yeah, I'm ready, we've been cooped up all day pretty much." She chuckled.

"Aw, you know you don't have to be. I have your back whenever you go out," he said as they walked down the hall.

"Thanks, but I felt weird about bothering you," she said sheepishly.

"It's my job." He laughed. "You're not like anyone I've guarded before."

"How many people *have* you guarded before?" she asked him curiously.

"Well, after the military, I've been doing this for about eight years now. Clients come and go, only a few were long-term. I had almost fifty clients," he told her.

"Do you like it?" She knew that she wouldn't like a job following or driving people around, waiting to beat someone up for them if need be.

"Ah… most days yes, when there's *something* to do," he said pointedly and Layla giggled.

"All right, tomorrow I promise to go out," she said and he quirked a brow at her. "Promise!" She laughed.

"All right then, miss," he said with a nod and then the elevator opened out to the garage and they were on the way to Dominique's. When they got to his block, Layla had to gasp.

"There's more people here than before," she said with wide eyes. She tried not to look out at them as they got close to Dominique's gate. John had to fight his way through the people who were ready to block the car to get a good shot. LJ started crying as he took in all the commotion, and by then, John got out of the car to clear people away, threatening to call the police. They cleared away quickly and John got back into the car to continue driving through.

"That was intense," Layla said as she was getting Lucas out of the car.

132

"Believe it or not, that wasn't as bad as it could be," John answered.

They used the kitchen door to get inside—it was unlocked. As soon as they were inside, Layla heard Isabelle and Dominique arguing. John stood by the kitchen door while Layla hesitated, wondering if she should go into the dining room.

"Why not? It's *obvious*. It's so obvious, Dominique. How long will it take for you to think 'LJ' needs a car?"

"Isabelle, can you please? I told you already, she hasn't *asked* me for anything," Dominique said angrily.

"I think you're smart enough to detect coercion, Dominique," she said sharply. "I still say you should just take custody of Lucas and give her a check and NDA so she doesn't say anything to the media. That's that, all of this would be over."

Layla was shocked to hear Isabelle say that outright to Dominique. What's more is she was afraid of what Dominique would say.

"I cannot believe you would actually suggest that. I would *never* take Lucas away from his mother, nor would I 'pay her off' to keep her out of our lives. If you can't get your shit together and start accepting that both Layla and Lucas will be in our lives, then maybe you shouldn't be in *my* life," Dominique said with such heat to his voice Layla almost recoiled and she was in the other room.

There was a smash and Layla gasped when she saw Isabelle storm around the corner and hurry through the kitchen without even looking up. John had just enough time to step aside before getting run down by her. When the door slammed shut, he and Layla shared a wide eyed glance. He mouthed the word 'wow' before Dominique slowly walked in.

"How long were you here?" he asked her slowly, his eyes glancing over her shoulder to John.

"I heard a lot," she said slowly.

"Don't listen to her. I'd never even consider doing that to you, believe me. I know that Lucas needs his mother and you need him, too," he said sincerely.

Layla did know that Dominique understood that after having to leave his own mother to live in a country an ocean away.

"Okay… I believe you," Layla said and she gestured to LJ who was complaining, still in his stroller. Dominique bent down to scoop him up, putting on a smile for Lucas.

"There's food in the dining room," he said and Layla followed him through the archway to the other room.

"Crap, I forgot about this…" he sighed.

Isabelle had smashed a plate on the ground and the mess was still there. Layla took LJ while Dominique got a broom to sweep up the mess.

"You know, sometimes... I swear she doesn't want things to work out between us." He sighed.

Layla had sat down at the table and was reaching for one of the Chinese takeout boxes to see what was inside.

"Do you want it to work out?" she asked.

Her heart was pounding as she waited for his answer, and she tried hard not to think about why. Why she was holding her breath and hoping like hell he'd say no?

"Sometimes..." was all he said, and Layla felt her chest tighten.

That was basically a maybe. The one word that wormed its way into a yes or no decision and drove people mad. Unconsciously, Layla rubbed her chest, then went about doling out some food for herself.

"So I told my dad that you'd be coming with Lucas to Thanksgiving and he's excited, so is my step-mom," Dominique said as he joined Layla and LJ at the table.

"Really? That's great," she said with a small smile, hoping Dominique's family would be welcoming of her. "Do they know... what the media is saying about you and such?" she asked.

"Well, they are still mostly talking about Isabelle. But the focus is shifting; they're getting better pictures of you two," he said with a sigh. "Anyhow, my family couldn't care less about the media fluff. They'd just ask me and I'd tell them," he said simply.

"So what's going to be on the brunch menu?" she asked.

"A *lot,* actually." Dominique went to count off all the food being made or brought and Layla had to say she was amazed.

"So there's going to be a lot of people there?" she asked with wide eyes.

"Well, not too many people. Just the family," he said with a small shrug.

"Wow, then you guys can eat," she commented, which made him laugh.

"Last Thanksgiving, Tony and I simply had one macaroni casserole and baked chicken. It was just the two of us. Well, actually, three of us; I knew about LJ by then," she said. When Dominique didn't say anything or even chuckle, she looked up and saw him gazing at her intently. "What's wrong? What did I say?" she asked him.

"Nothing… it's just—you put things in perspective for me. All the time," he said softly and glanced down at LJ, who was drinking his dinner contentedly. "It's easy to forget about things. Especially how I grew up, you know, it all seems so far away now," he spoke thoughtfully and looked at Layla with a strange expression she couldn't decipher.

It was almost fond. For some reason, she didn't really like for him to feel fondness for her. She… well, she wanted more. When she shouldn't, she absolutely shouldn't.

"You know… when I saw you, I felt like… I don't know. You slowed things down for me, even at the last two minutes of the fourth quarter. I knew we'd have something and now…" He glanced down at LJ who reached up to touch his face.

Layla knew she was in trouble then, as much as she tried to ignore it. "The Dom" Johnson was one she knew she couldn't get over.

# *Chapter 6*

As soon as John backed out of Dominique's drive, Layla knew she shouldn't have stayed over with LJ. There were even *more* paparazzi outside of his house and she just knew what they'd say. Everything was innocent, though. Layla slept in the guest bedroom and LJ spent the night in his room. They had a nice family night, watched a couple of movies, LJ had managed to worm-wiggle his way across the floor. It was a normal night with just the three of them.

"So how bad of a mob have you been in before?" Layla asked John, trying to get her mind off of the press of bodies to the window and cameras flashing into the car. Thank goodness LJ's car seat had a hood she could pull up.

"Well, I've escorted a singer out of a concert before, let's just say she's from Houston, and that mob was *huge*."

Layla smiled; she knew exactly who he was talking about and figured she'd want to be nowhere near that kind of crowd.

"Are you usually this nice to all of your clients?"

"Well, I do have to be polite and professional. But you're different. You aren't like the other well-off folk," he said and glanced at her briefly through the rear view.

"I'm not well off. This is all Dominique," she said with a sigh.

John simply nodded and then focused fully on the road. When they got back to the hotel, Layla took some time to unwind from that ride. There were even some people at the Langham, trying to speak with her on their way from the garage to the elevator.

As much as she wanted to unwind, though, she couldn't help but turn on the TV. It was programed to open on a news channel and indeed the morning show was talking about her and Dominique, less about Isabelle. Someone had gotten a really clear picture of Layla and Lucas, she was holding him next to John's car, about to put him into the stroller.

"So we've *finally*, finally got Dominique's mystery son's name. along with his mother's name. Clearly, in this picture, The Dom should have been there with them; they would have made a beautiful family. There's little baby Lucas with his mom, Layla Anderson, both names we learned from a close source on Dominique's end. Still, this Layla is a mystery, though, as is her adorable son who is very obviously Dom's. We still don't know for sure if an official paternity test has been done though…" The woman turned to her co-host to talk about the picture some more before they moved on to other news about another celebrity.

Layla was shocked. How'd they get her name? Her *full* name? She was about to do some searching on Google when the hotel phone started to ring.

"Hello?" she answered, wondering who was calling, and why.

139

"Hello, Miss Anderson, there's a visitor in the lobby for you. Your security measures require us to get permission to send her up." The front desk woman told her it was Isabelle waiting and Layla had her sent up, though she felt very hesitant and wary about actually letting Isabelle up.

When she knocked on the door, Layla glanced back at LJ playing on the blanket in the living room before letting Isabelle in. She was dressed very expensively, not in pretty regular clothes that Layla had seen her wear before. She was all made up, too, her hair done in an expertly-tousled fashion. *Maybe she's going for an interview or something*, Layla wondered. Standing on the other side of that door, she was reminded of just who Isabelle was.

"Uh… hi, come in," Layla said and stood aside for her to walk in.

"Sorry to just drop in, but I didn't have your number. Plus, I'll be quick," she said and sent a sideways glance at LJ playing with his basketball.

"Sure, what's up?" Layla asked.

"I know that Lucas is your son and Dominique's son. That's fine, I have no problem with him being in his child's life. But to be completely honest, it's you I have a problem with. I know you came from nothing and had nothing. You're fishing for his money and you think you can steal him away from me through the baby. But it's not going to happen and I'll tell you why. Dominique loves me, he loves the baby, that much is obvious. But you can be easily cut off, just like he dropped you after your blip of a fling. When things calm down between us like they always do, he'll see that you're just extra baggage causing trouble. He only tolerates you now because the baby is so young."

With that, she sent one glance at Lucas before giving one venomous look of disgust to Layla and turning on her heel to walk out, before she opened the door though, she glanced at Layla over her shoulder.

"I'd tread lightly if I were you is all. It wouldn't be that hard to convince him to take custody once the paternity test is had."

With that Isabelle left, leaving cold air in her wake. Layla took several deep breaths and walked back to LJ. She tried her hardest not to let Isabelle's words get to her, but they did and she couldn't help the few tears that fell onto her cheeks. It was all too much for her, having a bodyguard, for Pete's sake, living in what had to be a ridiculously expensive hotel, having an angry popstar verbally abuse her. It wasn't what she signed on for. All she wanted was for LJ to have his father in his life, something she never had.

At seeing Layla cry, LJ started to pout. She quickly wiped her face and put on a smile for him before he started to cry, which would only make her cry even more and it'd just be a big mess.

"Are we going to try crawling one more time?" She looked at Lucas who was staring at her as he held himself up in a half push up.

"Come on, just move that little chunky leg forward…" She smiled at him and held out her arms. He gave her a big toothless grin and moved his leg forward, still in a seated position and trying to wiggle his way over to her.

"You're getting it." She laughed as she picked him up, he was all giggles and squeals, and peppered him with kisses. "We have to get you some more sophisticated toys, some 'almost crawling' toys," she said and then realized what she said. It wasn't like she had any money to spare for something he didn't need, but Dominique did. So when she said "we" she really meant him. Was it some habit that was forming out of his generosity? Or did she really have the fact that he was one of the most well-paid athletes in the world in the back of her mind when she set out to tell Dominique about LJ? More than simply wanting Dominique in LJ's life?

Lucas reached down toward his toys and she let him play, watchful that he was then more mobile than he used to be. She pulled out her phone and did a search on herself. A lot of tabloid articles popped up. There were a few mean ones calling her a "no name gold digger," others simply said she was a "mystery woman" out to try and win Dominique away from Isabelle. There was one magazine site that actually had pictures from when she and Dominique first met. It showed him talking to her after the game and then a few pictures of her holding LJ, a clear view of them both. The article also went on to mention how Dominique hasn't yet posted anything to his social media about Lucas or Layla, effectively trying to keep things private.

After seeing a few more articles, Layla had enough; she probably shouldn't have opened that Pandora's Box anyway. She glanced down at Lucas who had rolled over to his back and was staring at her while sucking on about four of his fingers.

"I bet you're going to be just as athletic as your dad. Already trying to figure out how to crawl." She smiled at him and he grinned in return. "How about we go out for a bit?" she suggested.

LJ simply stared at her and she called John up and he was at the door in no time.

"We getting out of here?" he asked her and she nodded, giving him a small smile. "Hey, what's up?"

"Nothing... I just, uh, had a visit from Isabelle," Layla said, her voice wavering a bit and she hated that.

She wasn't exactly weak, but she wasn't one for confrontation or mean words. Her mother didn't raise her that way.

"Shit, I should have never even let the front desk call to let her up..."

"It's not your fault. She's just... going through a lot," Layla said and focused on getting LJ's bag together. Lucas was waiting patiently in his stroller, his pacifier in his mouth.

"Don't make excuses. I mean, c'mon, we both heard their arguments—she's not a nice person. You don't deserve her venom," he said adamantly. "Dominique shouldn't stand for that sort of vibe around his child either."

Layla simply blinked at John, wondering how much he cared about her and Lucas, she thought they were just a job to him. But he was visibly upset for her and looked like he wanted to put a fist through the wall.

"I'm fine, I'll get over it." She sighed.

He simply shook his head and sighed. "It's just not fair," he said and glanced over at LJ who grinned at him.

"So I was thinking we can go to a park somewhere? Somewhere away from Langham and the Near West side, so that there's less chance of being photographed," she suggested.

"I know the perfect place; it'll be a bit of a drive though."

Layla told him that was fine and went to get a good jacket for LJ. They made it to the car hastily, before any of the media people milling about the hotel and garage could spot them. While on the way to John's perfect park, Layla got a call from an unknown number and she hesitated before answering it. The security program Dominique installed marked the number as "safe" so she answered, though cautiously.

"Hello?"

"Ah, hi is this… Layla Anderson?" She didn't recognize the tentative male voice. Whoever it was sounded nice enough though.

"Can I ask who's calling?" she said and John glanced at her briefly through the rear view mirror.

"Of course, but um… this may come as a shock to you. I'm Clifford Anderson… your father." Layla's jaw dropped and her eyes widened probably to the size of saucers.

John pulled the car over into the parking lot of a CVS and he actively listened in on the phone call, sending Layla an inquiring glance.

"I—I'm sorry? I… I don't know my father," she said numbly. Her lips actually felt numb and the rest of her body really cold. "How did you get my number?"

"Well, the method was really unethical, but the result is that I… finally got a hold of you." He sighed in relief it sounded like.

"I've never heard of a… Clifford Anderson. My mother never mentioned the name," she said, still numb with shock and shaking a little at that. She glanced at John, who was suddenly just as wide-eyed as she was. "Who are you?" she asked him slowly.

"Your mother knew me as Cali, it was a nickname I had back then. I'm not sure if you've heard of me, but I own a software company operating out of California."

Layla wouldn't know anything about that. She glanced at John again—clearly he knew who Clifford Anderson was.

145

"But I don't understand… you *knew* about me?" she asked him, incredulous.

"I knew your mother was pregnant and I knew her name. But when she left, she didn't leave any way for me to find her. Plus, I'm sure you lived relatively off the grid because of your situation. Until all of this with Dominique Johnson."

"She left you?" Layla was having a hard time computing much of anything, all she kept slamming into was confusion and shock.

"I can explain more if you'd agree to meet. I'm in Chicago, actually. I'll come to you wherever you are. Just please, give me a chance to explain myself. I'm sure your mother told you about why she left." He sounded so remorseful and Layla could tell that he desperately wanted a meeting with her.

"I… um…" She glanced at John who was still staring at her, openly curious.

"Sure, okay. LJ and I were just heading to…" John told her the name of the park and Clifford told her he'd be there within twenty minutes.

She ended the call and stared at John, who watched her sort of expectantly.

"Who is Clifford Anderson?"

"His company makes the craziest future tech you could imagine. They're known for their huge government contracts. You know how the military always gets the tech you see in movies before it trickles down to the public? Well, that's him, he's one of the modern geniuses of the world… not to mention pretty high up on Forbes' most wealthy list."

"I've never even heard of him," she murmured.

"People who have anything to do with the military certainly have. He's not Iron Man, but Tony Stark? More like it." John put the car in gear and backed out of the CVS. Layla pretended to understand his analogy; she'd only seen one Iron Man movie and that was a long time ago. "Now that I think about it… you look a lot like him," John said with a quick glance at her through the rear view mirror. "This is the best job ever," he said and that made Layla smile. Though only briefly—she was riddled with nerves.

"I feel like I'm going to throw up…" she said the closer they got to Lincoln Park. Never in her lifetime did she imagine she'd meet her father, regardless of what he did or who he was.

"Don't worry. If it helps, Clifford always seems like a down-to-earth guy, from interviews I've watched," John offered.

Layla glanced over at LJ, he was trying to eat one of his rattles, cute as ever.

"How'd you feel when you met your dad for the first time?" she asked him. He simply gurgled happily at her. She sighed—he was no help.

"We're here," John said.

Once they parked, they slowly made their way to the garden. It was very well manicured and not too crowded, so it was easy for someone who recognized Layla to walk up to them. John trailed behind her and LJ, of course, just as a precaution. Layla sat down on a nearby bench and glanced around for some landmarks in case Clifford called her cell again. She couldn't help but glance this way and that as she waited. She was so close to just blowing the whole thing and going to the zoo like John suggested earlier.

"We should go, I'm too nervous. Plus, what if it's some elaborate setup?"

She turned to glance at John whose eyes were wide as he looked over her shoulder. She turned back around and saw a stately man, walking determinedly her way. He was tall, maybe six-foot-three, and seemed to have an athletic physique. His eyes were light brown like hers, and his curly hair was styled into a neat brush cut. He was a little lighter in skin tone than Layla, but some of his features resembled hers, like his ears and well-formed cheekbones. He was a very handsome man, angular jaw, slightly cleft chin, and a perfect brow. She certainly saw why her mother might have been initially attracted to him. He was wearing a light windbreaker and jeans, and he looked like a regular guy. His sunglasses were folded on his button down shirt and he seemed relaxed with his hands in his pockets.

"Is that him?" she whispered to John.

"It is…" he whispered back.

Layla stood up when Clifford was close enough. He stopped only a couple feet away from her.

"Layla…" he said with a small smile and slightly pained expression. "You look like me… and her," he said with a small chuckle.

"I can see the resemblance, too…" she said slowly.

Not to be ignored, LJ called out and Clifford looked down at him, a wide smile stretching across his lips. "And this is Lucas. He's beautiful."

"Thank you," she said a bit awkwardly.

Clifford's eyes glanced past Layla to John no doubt. He quickly introduced himself to Clifford, who seemed like he appreciated John's being there.

"It seems like Dominique is taking care of you," he said, pleased.

"Taking care of LJ," Layla said. "It's complicated I guess," she added.

"We have much to talk about," he said and gestured for her to walk with him. She pushed LJ's stroller and began a slow stroll with Clifford.

"So I imagine your mother told you some bad things about me," he started.

149

Layla found that she liked his voice; it had a warmth to it and he definitely seemed sincere.

"She didn't tell me anything about you. All she *did* tell me was that she never told you about me. Because having you in my life would only bring unnecessary hardship, more than we already endured," Layla said.

"She didn't even tell you my name?" he asked incredulously.

"Nope, didn't want me to look you up even," Layla said, only then questioning her mom's judgement. "But why would she, I don't know, hate you that much?"

"Because I promised her so much and betrayed her when it came down to it. She has every right to hate me for what I did."

His voice grew thick with so much emotion it made Layla wonder what exactly happened between he and her mother.

"I was on the cusp of really getting my company going, of signing my first big contract and I told her I'd give her the world. That it would just be me and her. Back then, I was back and forth between Chicago and California and she was ready to leave our hometown to live with me on the west coast. I thought I was ready, too, but then someone got into my head. I *let* them make me think that I could accomplish so much more and be so much better without a wife and the need to settle down on my mind. I believed them and I never made the trip back to Chicago to get her. Then I get a voice mail one day, her sister telling me that she was pregnant and the baby was mine. I chose not to believe her. I chose to believe that she was trying to trap me into seeing your mom again and I thought I didn't want that. I thought I wanted success more than anything. I had the wrong people around me.

"Growing up on the South Side, living poor, you have that drive like a sickness and it can ruin people if they're not careful." He shook his head; his voice had gone a bit hoarse from the emotion he was holding in. "Maybe your mother was right in not wanting me in your life back then, I wouldn't have been any good. But I've realized that I can't go through life alone and if you were real, that I had to do everything in my power to make things right. With you and your mother."

"Clifford... my mom passed away from cancer years ago," Layla told him, as it seemed like he didn't know.

Clifford actually stumbled a bit. John rushed forward to steady him just in time and Layla stopped walking. She glanced around for a bench and took Clifford's hand to sit him down. She supposed she should have told him while he was sitting.

"*What?*"

"She passed away when I was seventeen. My aunt died of cancer, too, when I was much younger," she said, and he simply stared at her with wide eyed shock and horror.

"And you've lived... on your own? Since you were seventeen?" he asked incredulously.

"I had my cousin Tony, but yeah we had to rough it for some time," she said and brushed her hair from her face.

"I'm so sorry, Layla… I'm so, so sorry," he said, his voice cracked and wavering.

He pinched the bridge of his nose, his shoulders drooping, and head hung low. Layla watched him cry for her mom, for the love he once had and lost sight of. She felt bad for him, she really did, though she felt she should be upset with him, for hurting her mom like that. It seemed like he changed from the man he described, though, which was hard to deny as he was crying so openly.

"It's all right, Clifford, I forgive you. And I think she forgave you, too, a long time ago," Layla put her hand on his shoulder and he took a deep, shaky breath. "As long as you really have changed…" she added.

"I have, I—I always felt that my learning about you was an act of fate, but maybe it was Lori, maybe she finally thought I was worthy enough to know you," he said, his voice still sad.

"I'd like to think that," Layla said and rubbed his shoulder comfortingly.

"So will you allow me to be in your life? In Lucas' too?" he asked tentatively.

"Of course you can," she said without hesitation. For the first time in a while, she felt light and, well, happy, excited to finally get to know her real father. Briefly, she forgot all about Isabelle and the drama Dominique was bringing into her life. "We were headed to the zoo if you'd like to come," she offered.

"Without a doubt," he said and gave her a small smile. "You're like your mother you know… so good and kind," he told her.

She felt warmth spread through her and couldn't help but smile a bit bashfully.

"Thank you, that means a lot," she said as they stood up.

"So tell me about yourself, you must be… what, twenty-three, twenty-four?"

"I'm twenty-four."

"Do you have a career, or still in school?" he asked.

"Well, I've been saving up for school, I'll be ready to start applying soon," she told him.

"Did you finish high school after your mother passed?"

"No, I took care of her when she got sick and had to drop out. I got my GED, though, so technically, I did finish," she said.

"How long have you had to work?" he asked her slowly.

"Probably since I was eleven. I babysat, then moved on to working as a stock girl or bagger then, eventually, I started working at a local diner. Until it closed down recently."

He asked her more about what she was doing and Layla explained how she was sort of in limbo until she and LJ were settled in the house Dominique bought.

"You know I would be happy to pay for your school and take care of you. Help you get on your feet," he offered.

She glanced at him warily, but he had a determined expression that gave her pause.

"I kind of want to make it on my own, you know? Simply having Dominique do all he's done for us already is almost unbearable..."

Clifford shook his head adamantly.

"I'm your father, Layla. I can understand how you'd feel strange with Dominique paying for things, but he's taking care of his son. Let *me* help *you*."

Layla bit her lip; she was conflicted, especially after the accusations of Isabelle and what some tabloids were saying about her.

"Anything you need: we'll get you enrolled in a school and you can go ahead to pursue whatever you want."

Layla didn't know what to say, she felt overwhelmed.

"I don't know what to say... I'm just, I'm really overwhelmed," she admitted.

Before they walked into the zoo area, Clifford took her into a hug and Layla felt strangely at home. She always figured that if she ever met her father she'd only say two words to him and that was that. He was right, she had more of her mom in her than she realized and readily forgiving someone really worked wonders.

"Thank you, Clifford," she said softly.

"You can call me Cliff or, you know, Dad," he chuckled.

"I'll start with Cliff for now," she said and they both laughed.

Their day wasn't too bad, it was only a little awkward when Cliff insisted on paying for everything. Otherwise, they had a great time at the zoo. Lucas was wide-eyed and giggly the whole time. He really enjoyed seeing the lions and Cliff bought him a stuffed animal, of course.

By the time they got back to the hotel, it was pretty late, LJ was asleep even as Layla transferred him from car seat to stroller. When she got upstairs, Clifford and John in tow, they were talking about something or other concerning Cliff's latest project. Layla was surprised to see Dominique was at the suite, waiting for her.

"Hey, I was just about to call you. You're Clifford Anderson," he said, his eyes locking on Cliff, then they slid to Layla and back to Cliff. "Are the two of you related?"

"One good thing about being on the media radar is that my father found me," Layla said and Dominique's jaw fell slack.

"It's good to meet you, sir." He shook Cliff's hand and Layla glanced at him while he appraised Dominique.

"Nice to meet you, too. Lucas is going to look a lot like you when he gets older," Cliff said.

"So what's up?" Layla asked Dominique before he could respond.

"Uh… well, the house is finally ready," he said, studying Layla closely.

"Oh, so we can check out then?" she asked.

She couldn't exactly make eye contact with him. She partly blamed him for Isabelle's appearance earlier regardless of whether he deserved the blame or not.

"Yeah, and see everything. It looks like Lucas will have to wake up surprised though." He smiled at LJ, asleep in the stroller.

Layla didn't really respond. She told them that she'd get her stuff together as well as LJ's and retreated to the bedrooms to pack.

"Hey, do you need me to take anything to the car?" John poked his head into the room and Layla nodded with a grateful smile.

"Yeah, I think I have everything packed up. These are all good to go," she gestured to her suitcases. She was packing the last of LJ's things into his own bag.

"Thanks, John," she said with a warm smile, which he returned.

Just then, Dominique poked his head into the room, his eyes almost suspicious as he glanced at John squeezing out with the bags.

"Is everything okay?" he asked her. "You must have had a big day, meeting your father and all. He's a great guy, but I'm sure you must be feeling all… weird," he said, his accent coloring his words more heavily than normal.

"Yeah, everything is fine. Cliff is great," Layla said in a clipped tone. She finished with LJ's bag and took a deep breath. "Did you see the house yet?" she asked him, wanting to escape his scrutiny.

"Yeah… it's perfect," he said and she stepped out to walk to the living room.

Cliff was rocking LJ's stroller back and forth, smiling at him. It warmed Layla's heart. All at once it seemed, he had his dad and granddad in his life, though Cliff hardly looked old enough to be called grandpa.

"We're ready to go," Layla said and Cliff looked up.

"Great, he looks like he needs a bed," he said with a chuckle.

As soon as John got back they headed out. Layla was excited to see the house, but less excited to be around Dominique, though she knew she shouldn't blame him and should just explain things. She was still too hurt by Isabelle's words.

"Oh my goodness. The house is perfect!" Layla said when they arrived inside.

It reflected the outside: the interior was decorated in inviting pastel shades and light-colored furniture. Where it was warm on the outside, it was light and welcoming on the inside. The house wasn't too girly inside, which Layla liked, and the furniture was all modern without being too contemporary and stiff. She explored upstairs and fell in love with LJ's second new room. It was done in the same engaging colors as his room at Dominique's.

"So do you like it, the whole house and everything?" Dominique surprised her. He had come up with LJ, putting him to bed.

"It's a dream; I can't thank you enough," she said sincerely, though she still felt reticent around him.

"It's like I said before, it's what I'm supposed to do."

Layla watched him change LJ gingerly, as not to wake him too much. She left him to put Lucas to bed and went to find Cliff. He was up in the library, taking a look at the book shelves.

"Dominique did well, this is a nice place," Cliff said. "Though we should do some book shopping. Do you like to read?" he asked her.

"Ah, sometimes. I've never really gotten into reading much," she admitted sheepishly. "How long are you staying in Chicago?"

"Two weeks. Did you have any Thanksgiving plans?"

158

Layla thought about Dominique's invitation and she sighed.

"Yeah, but more and more I'm thinking of skipping those plans," she said rather morosely.

"How come?"

"Hey, Layla, Lucas is in his crib. I'm going to head home." Dominique appeared at the head of the staircase. It didn't seem like he overheard she and Cliff talking, though.

"Okay, then, see you," she said and he gave her and Cliff a nod before he was gone.

"So yeah, Dominique invited me to his dad's for Thanksgiving brunch, but his fiancée said some really mean things to me and I just don't know if I'd feel right being around all of his family and especially her." She sighed.

"I understand now. And yeah, I wouldn't put myself in that situation either. But have you spoken to him about it?" Cliff looked at her expectantly.

She shook her head no. "I just feel so jumbled up when it comes to him. I can't take it. I think maybe I just need a break or something."

"So why don't you let him have Lucas for a couple of hours on Thanksgiving and we can do something simple? Have a dinner out at a nice restaurant, just the two of us."

Layla gave him a small smile and nodded. "Yeah, that sounds nice," she said, some of the tension in her chest dissipating. A huge yawn escaped her chest and she covered her mouth in surprise. "Oh wow, I didn't realize I was so tired." She chuckled.

"It is pretty late. How about I come by tomorrow?" he asked tentatively.

"Sure, that'd be great!"

"Good, then we can look at schools and such," he said with a pointed smile, and Layla nodded with a chuckle.

"Definitely. It's a plan," she said and then walked him out.

John took him back to his hotel, then it was just her and sleeping LJ in their brand new house. She wandered into the living room, equipped with a nice view of the quaint street and comfortable furniture, not to mention a nice gas fireplace. Layla checked the time and hoped Tony would still be awake, though it was nearly eleven-thirty. She Skype called him and he actually answered.

"Layla! I was just thinking about you," he said with a huge smile.

"Oh my goodness, Tony, let me look at you!" she said. He was definitely a lot healthier than his days living without a home. He had some lean muscle on his bones and was the handsome Tony she grew up with. The one that had women turning their heads from miles away. "You're looking a little too sexy over there in Maryland," she said, making him laugh.

"I could say the same for you, but then again, you've always looked good. So how are you? Where are you now?" he asked as he took in her new background.

"Oh I have to give you a tour. This is the new house," she said and proceeded to take him through all the rooms and floors of the house.

"So I have some news for you, are you sitting?" she asked him when she made it back to her seat on the sofa chair.

"What's up?"

"My father reached out to me," she said, getting it all out there.

"Holy shit!" he said, his face an expression of pure surprise.

"Yeah, he saw my picture and heard my name from the media following us around. He flew to Chicago and looked up my number. Simply gave me a call and we met!"

"Just like that? What's the story? Why'd your mom not want you knowing about him?"

Layla filled him in on who Cliff was and his reaction was largely like hers.

"That's some craziness," he breathed in shock after she finished her story.

"Yeah, apparently he's well known for what he does. But before today, I'd never heard of him. I don't follow the business world," she admitted.

"It's kind of hard when all you had was generic news channels and a Roku stick that barely worked for Netflix," Tony scoffed.

"That thing lasted the test of time, I still have it somewhere… Well, I will after I unpack." Layla glanced at the suitcases sitting in the living room. She was too lazy to move them.

"Yeah, it was a trooper, so was your old landlord for lending his WiFi to us for so long." Tony chuckled.

Layla realized she never said goodbye to Landlord Larry. She made a mental note to send him a letter. After catching up with Tony some more, they ended the call and she went upstairs to sleep in her huge new master bedroom. It was hard to fall asleep; the sheets were too new and the bed way too big. Maybe once she found a job and got settled with that and school, she could get a dog, one that would grow up with LJ.***

Layla spent several days with her dad and LJ if he wasn't with Dominique. She was coming to trust him more and more with LJ and was actually glad to be spending less time with Dominique, who always seemed in the company of Isabelle these days. Layla managed to skip Thanksgiving with him under the guise of getting to know her father and spending time with him, which she did really want to do. And they had gotten the whole birth certificate thing taken care of after Thanksgiving as well.

Cliff helped her get into one of the better and more well-known physical therapy schools. She'd be starting come spring and she had plenty of time to find a job that suited her. Something that wasn't in the restaurant business. She was tired of serving plates.

Layla was sitting in the library with LJ while he played in his play pen. The alarm sounded for the front door, alerting her that someone was home. She checked the time and wondered if it was Cliff or Dominique. Dom wasn't due to pick LJ up for another hour.

"Hello, hello?" Dominique called up and she heard his footsteps on the stairs.

"You're carly!" Layla called and he found them upstairs.

"You both look so studious," he smirked.

"I was just applying for some office jobs," she said, almost sheepishly.

"That's good, something better than working in a restaurant. Though you know, you don't *have* to…"

"I don't have to work, between you and my father it's cnough. I want to. I want to feel productive," she said, a bit sharper with him than she intended.

"What's up with you? How come I haven't seen you in like a week? And every time I do see you, you act like this?"

"You really don't know? She hasn't said anything to you all this time?" Layla asked him.

"What are you talking about? Isabelle?"

"She came to the hotel and basically told me to walk on thin ice when around you. That you'd easily just drop me if you wanted. That you *would*," she said.

"She came to you with that? In front of LJ?" he asked in a deadly calm voice.

"Yes."

Dominique began shaking his head. He glanced at LJ then back at Layla, his eyes sweeping the length of her. For some reason she felt his gaze was different, her skin tingled seemingly everywhere his eyes touched. Then he really surprised her by pulling her tightly against him and sealing his lips over hers. She let out a small gasp of surprise, but his arms only tightened around her and she melted into the kiss. She had almost forgotten how soft his lips were.

"I'll be back," he said in a hoarse whisper and kissed her softly once more before he left.

She simply stared at the space he once stood, wide eyed in shock. She definitely didn't see that happening.

# *Chapter 7*

Layla was at a loss for what to do next. She supposed she should continue applying to jobs, but she was in shock. What was he going to do? Break up with Isabelle? But then what would that mean? Did he kiss her because he wanted to get together with her? She rubbed the back of her neck and glanced at LJ. He was lying on his back and kicking his legs happily while he chewed on one of his toys. She sighed and sat back down at the desk. She glanced at the computer and, of course, went to Google.

What she found on Dominique and Isabelle was a bit shocking. The media had transitioned from her and LJ to Dominique and Isabelle's relationship. Apparently, they've been arguing more than ever and sometimes in public. There was even a cell phone video of them having a heated conversation at a restaurant. Everyone seemed to think their relationship wouldn't pick up again if they broke up once more. She did a search on herself and found that it was well known already that her father was Clifford Anderson. There were plenty of pictures of them around the city with LJ. Some speculated whether Layla had his smarts or not. She had considered it herself at one point, but didn't think too far into it. She supposed she was good at math when she was in school. But she didn't think she had an IQ as high as her father's.

Layla went back to checking on her applications and e-mail. Nothing back yet. Her phone started to ring and she held her breath, wondering if it was Dominique. It was Tony calling.

"Oh my goodness Tony," she answered. "You will *not* believe what just happened."

"What happened?" he chuckled.

"Dominique kissed me," she said and he paused on the other line.

"He *what*?"

Layla explained what happened. She was talking in fast forward because she was still in shock over the whole thing.

"Holy shit, Layla…" he said when she was done.

"Yeah, and I'm still in shock."

"So, apart from that, how's the job search going?"

She heard him bite into something on the other line, maybe an apple.

"Can you not crunch in my ear?" she asked and he laughed.

"Sorry, but I've been staring at this apple for hours and finally got the time to sit down and eat it." He chuckled.

"The job search is a little dry. I think the fact that Cliff is my dad is hindering me in some way. Maybe the employers don't think I really *need* a job."

"So why don't you work for him?" Tony suggested casually.

"I don't know anything about his company. Also he doesn't have a branch or anything in Chicago," she said.

"You'd be surprised; just ask him," he suggested.

"So how is work for you? You're busier and busier these days." She got up to get Lucas out of his play pen—it was time to feed him.

"Yeah, work is great, Layla. A dream. I'm like the boss over here and everyone I work with is great. The office is running smoothly and the guy over me is really glad I moved to Maryland. Said I have skills," he said immodestly and Layla laughed.

"You're such a dork," she chuckled.

"You know, soon I'll be living like you. They reward good work ethic here."

Layla was so glad to hear he was doing well in Maryland.

"Does that mean you'll get to visit home soon?" she asked.

She missed her cousin dearly and she knew LJ would love to see him.

"I'll see what I can do. Maybe I can spare a weekend soon," he promised her.

She was about to make sure he would come when she heard the door again. It had to be Dominique back already.

"Okay, you'd better. I'll talk to you soon, cousin," she said and quickly ended the call.

She got up just as Dominique came jogging up the steps.

"Wait, wait… This is perfect. Don't move," he said and then pulled out his phone. "Smile."

She slowly smiled, still confused as to why he was taking a picture. He snapped one of her holding LJ, who was actually smiling at the camera, or his dad rather. Dominique smiled as he looked at the photo and he walked over to show Layla.

"Why'd you take a picture of us?"

"It's time I stop trying to appease Isabelle. I ended things with her. She's a jealous woman who is only out for her own best interest. She throws fits when she sees things not going her way. I'm done with her. I've outgrown her."

"So why'd you take the picture?" she asked and he laughed, putting an arm around her and LJ. "To post it to my Instagram and end all this media speculation."

He led them downstairs and Layla went to look for a bottle for LJ. She realized she didn't restock his breast milk and he had run out of formula as well.

"We have to make a grocery run," she murmured.

Before if she'd been low on food, it was simply because she didn't have enough money to go food shopping. Then it was only so because she'd simply not paid much attention to it. Again, she was amazed in the shift of focus she had when the simple necessities in life were taken care of.

She went to join Dominique in the family room and grabbed one of LJ's blankets that were laying around.

"Look."

Dominique showed her his phone and she first noticed how many likes from Instagram he was getting. Then she looked at the picture—good thing she was still dressed from the day in an oversized sweater and tights, though she only had socks on. LJ was cute as ever, his dimple showing and wearing a blue pajama onesie. The caption he wrote said, "My family no matter what. This is me."

Layla simply smiled—she didn't know what to say.

"Now I'm going to load all those cute pictures I've been taking of LJ," he said eagerly.

Layla laughed and touched his hand briefly.

"How about you only load a couple? That's also used for work," she reminded him. He simply grumbled a bit and she limited him to four pictures. After that she got to breast feeding LJ as he started to remind her what she was supposed to be doing.

"This may sound odd, but can I see?" Dominique asked her slowly when he realized she was breast feeding Lucas.

She chuckled and looked at him curiously.

"Why do you want to see?"

"Because I've never seen it in real life and I'm just curious," he said with a sheepish chuckle.

Layla took a breath and removed the blanket. Dominique studied LJ for a moment and Layla couldn't help but to laugh.

"Okay, I see how it works," he said and she laughed again.

"You're too much," she chuckled as he covered her up again with the blanket. "So…um…" She wanted to ask him more about Isabelle. He was in an oddly good mood after just breaking off his engagement. He looked at her expectantly and she chewed on her lip, trying to decide if she should just come up with some lame cover up.

"We've been arguing since I told her about you and LJ, worse than we ever have, Layla. It was never going to work between us. I'm just glad not to be around her negative, sucking energy any longer." He sighed, mostly in relief, and stretched out on the couch.

"Well, I'm happy for you then. Everyone deserves to be happy," she said sincerely and rubbed his shoulder.

She really wanted to ask him about that kiss, but figured that was enough talk for the night. One couldn't push a guy on opening up all at once.

"Yeah, and whether she realizes it or not, she's better off without me too," he murmured. "Oh, the next few basketball games are going to be at home, you're invited you know. You, LJ, and whoever else. You can bring Cliff if you want to."

"Oh and John? I sort of made a bet with him that I lost and I have to get him into a game," she said with a chuckle.

Dominique quirked a brow at her, a slight frown on his face.

"Sure…" he murmured, then pursed his lips almost suspiciously. "Are you and John close or something?"

"Yeah, I'd like to think we're friends. I mean, it's kind of weird for me to have someone drive me around and follow me around and not know anything about him," she said.

"Friends. Huh." He sat up as Layla was moving LJ around and putting her boob back into her shirt.

She started to pat LJ's back and gave Dominique a curious look.

"I'm not allowed to be friends with John?" she asked him.

"Of course, it's just that, you know. You're…" he shrugged, almost pouting and Layla had to hide her smile.

"I'm what? Likeable?" she teased him. "Likeable and able to make friends outside of my family?"

"Of course you're likeable. You're loveable actually," he said and turned her chin toward him. She almost held her breath, but he simply kissed her on the cheek. Confused, Layla focused on burping LJ. "So will you come to the game tomorrow? Please?"

"Sure, of course we'll be there." She smiled at him.

"Yes! Finally, he'll see me play," he said excitedly then started talking to LJ in his baby voice, telling him how cool the stadium would be.

"I don't know if he'll be able to handle the noise though," Layla realized.

"We can get him some headphones, no problem," Dom said excitedly.

"So we'll like… meet your teammates and such?" Layla asked him a little nervously.

"Sure, they've been bothering me about seeing LJ for a while now." He smirked. "So how is the job search going?"

"It's hard on this side of town, or maybe just because everyone knows I'm Cliff's daughter and don't really need a job as badly as other people do."

"You know you don't *have* to work," Dominique said and she glared at him. "Okay, I'm sorry." He chuckled.

"I talked to Tony earlier and he suggested working for my dad maybe, but I don't think he has anything connected to his company in Chicago," she said.

"He does, several think tank offices and a prototype lab," Dominique said expertly.

"How do you know?" she asked him incredulously.

"Because he told me. I asked him what business he had in the city." He shrugged.

Layla and Cliff hardly talked about his work; he was always far more interested in her and her life, in LJ and Tony, things like that.

"I guess I could talk to him tomorrow then," she said and texted Cliff about the basketball game. He sent a message right back saying he'd love to go.

LJ had fallen asleep while Layla was burping him, but he let out a surprise belch that had him startled awake. He looked at Layla with wide shocked eyes and both she and Dominique burst into laughter. Lucas started to laugh, too, as if what happened was the funniest thing he'd ever seen.

Layla wiped tears from her eyes, but started laughing all over again when Lucas let out another little burp and cracked up all over again. Dominique was clutching his midsection he was laughing so hard.

"You've never burped like that before, huh, buddy?" He chuckled and kissed LJ on the head.

After they all calmed down from the giggles, LJ settled down, falling asleep on his own while Layla held him. She got up to go put him in his crib and Dominique followed her. Since LJ was asleep, Layla felt kind of awkward being alone with Dom.

"So uh… I'll see you tomorrow?" he asked her once they were out in the family room again.

"Yeah, we'll be at the game," she said and walked him to the door.

"I…" he turned to say something to her, but he trailed off and simply stared at her for a moment. "I'll see you tomorrow," was all he ended up saying and then made a hasty exit out to the gate.

Layla closed the door and took a deep breath. What was all of that about? She took another deep breath, knowing she was in for a doozy with Dominique. But she didn't want to be played with, that was for sure. If he wanted her, he should be decisive. It wasn't nice to confuse someone like that, especially as the mother of his child. With nothing better to do, she went upstairs to watch some TV until she fell asleep. But, of course, her mind was abuzz with speculation, wondering if she and Dominique could get together, like she's always wanted. Hell, she knew she had feelings for him, those never went away from their first little fling together. She forced herself to fall asleep and made sure to put LJ's baby monitor on her nightstand before she did.

Come morning, Layla woke up feeling pretty tired. Apparently, it was impossible to force yourself to sleep. LJ was awake and crying for being left alone too long. She got him ready for the day before getting ready herself. Cliff wanted to spend the day with them. He sent her a text earlier saying he needed a good break from work. She wondered how he'd feel talking about work, or her asking for a low level job at one of his branches.

"Are you ready to spend some time with grandpa today?" she asked LJ as she fixed herself some coffee and warmed up his breakfast. Cliff called her cell when he was outside. He had the code to walk right in, but he always called, unlike Dominique, which Layla couldn't really complain about—it was his house. She opened the door for Cliff. He was holding two takeout bags and had a cup of coffee in both hands.

"I hope you haven't eaten yet." He smiled.

"You're amazing. I was just about to put a pot of coffee on." She chuckled, letting him in.

"You don't use one of those K-cup things?" he asked her.

"No, I've always liked to scoop out the ground coffee, smell it, and get all excited for my cup to be brewed sort of the old-fashioned way," she said, making him laugh.

"So what are we doing today? Other than the basketball game, what are you feeling up for?"

"I'm not sure... Something fun, but it's getting kind of hard. The days keep getting colder and colder," Layla said, peeking into the takeout bags as Cliff unloaded French toast and various sides.

"We can think of something, I'm sure. Google knows all," he chuckled and Layla smirked. She was finding she had an unhealthy attachment to the convenience of Google.

"So uh…Cliff…" Layla felt a little awkward about actually asking for a job, but she had to try. She didn't want to end up not working and leeching off of Dominique and Cliff. "Dominique was telling me that you had a few branches or something like that in Chicago?"

"I do. I have a few smaller offices dedicated to coming up with practical tech ideas and readying those ideas to pitch to me to go further with it. I also have a prototype lab to help make things easier for those coming up with new ideas. Do you want a job?" he asked her readily, seeming like he was willing to pull some strings on the spot. "I can't believe I didn't think about this before. One of the think tank offices needs a new office assistant. I think it'll be perfect for you." He smiled. "I can't believe I hadn't thought of that. The job is yours, don't even think about it," he said and pulled out his phone.

Layla chuckled, she was learning Cliff's little quirks. Like his tendency to half-talk to himself and someone else.

"Are you sure I'm not keeping someone out of a job?"

"No, no, I just learned that the old office assistant got a job elsewhere, across the country. They haven't even posted the opening yet," he assured her.

"All right, then. Thanks, Cliff; this means a lot," she said with a smile and leaned over to kiss him on the cheek. He smiled at her, pleased with himself, and they all went back to having breakfast at the breakfast bar. LJ mostly held up the bottle on his own so Layla was able to eat while just holding him. She and Cliff decided to visit Shedd Aquarium with LJ, knowing he'd love it. Layla contemplated telling John about the basketball game, but after Dominique acting so weird, she decided to invite him to a game another time.

After they got back from nearly all day at the aquarium, Layla had to admit she was a little nervous to go to the game. She hadn't been to one since the game where they met. When she, LJ, and Cliff got back to her house, she saw that Dominique left them all jerseys. LJ's had "Little Dom" printed on the back over Dominique's number, the number eight.

"That's nice of him, but I'm not wearing that," Cliff said when he saw that one of the jerseys were meant for him.

"I have to agree with you," Layla chuckled. Cliff offered to change LJ into his new shirt while Layla did a quick change. Soon they were on the way to the stadium, John glancing to the back seat every so often, his expression a little pouty even though Layla explained to him why he should wait a few games before she makes good on her bet.

They pulled up to a less-crowded entrance of the arena and Layla was a little surprised that the stadium personnel already knew that she and LJ and Cliff were family of Dom. They were given arm bands and led up to the team family booth. Layla was relieved not to have LJ down with the loud crowd and cameras that circled around the floor seats.

"Oh my goodness, it's Dom's baby," someone squealed as soon as Layla and Cliff walked in with LJ.

She glanced around and saw the few people already there looking at her curiously. They found their seats, which was an entire row in the box. Layla pulled LJ out of the stroller and Cliff pushed it out of the way while she walked over to look down at the court. LJ put his hand on the glass as soon as he saw Dominique go out onto the court to warm up.

"Yeah, that's daddy," Layla said in his ear and he squealed happily. She kissed him on the cheek and turned around to sit with Cliff.

"You know, coming to more of these games you'll get to know more of the players' families and such," he said to her in a low voice.

She glanced around briefly and caught a few curious glances aimed her way.

"Yeah I guess so," she said with a small smirk, hoping that there would be nice and genuine people to meet there. People less like Isabelle.

"Cliff, how would you handle all this?" she asked him and he cracked up.

"Honestly? If I were you I'd just stay out of the whole social media black hole. You'll be fine that way," he assured her.

"Yeah, I'll leave that up to Dominique," she said and held LJ up on her lap.

He wanted to stretch his legs and reach over to Cliff's face. Once the game started, LJ would hardly let Layla sit down, which she had to apologize for, but she was pleasantly surprised to find that no one minded. A few moms were standing with their toddlers as well, so Layla was almost literally joining the club. Surprisingly, LJ loved to watch the basketball game and all the people below. After the game, they went downstairs to see Dominique and caught him just as he was giving an interview on the court. He grinned at Layla and LJ when he spotted them and waved, causing the woman interviewing him to glance back briefly.

"How'd he like it?" Dominique asked when he was done with the interview. He was all sweaty and still breathing a little hard.

"He loved it. He recognized you and never wanted to sit down," she said with a chuckle.

"That means he's going to be on the court soon!" he said as she handed LJ over.

"Is this the little man?" One huge player came out of nowhere, nearly scaring Layla to death. "Oh I'm sorry, miss." He chuckled and her eyes widened when she realized it was Neil Brown, another great player in the league.

"Yes, this is Lucas, you can finally stop bugging me," Dominique said and Neil made baby noises at LJ who hid his face

179

shyly. Soon there were more very tall men just off of the court crowding around and Layla had to make a brief exit.

"It's hard to breathe in that huddle," Layla said when she found Cliff.

He laughed, watching Dominique hold LJ up over his teammates who started singing that song from the beginning of *The Lion King*. Layla couldn't help but crack up. Meanwhile, LJ was simply loving the attention. After they were done, Dominique handed LJ over and told her to wait for him so they could grab dinner after his press conference. Layla sat in the still-emptying stadium and tried to get LJ to eat his dinner, but he was too excited to do his evening routine in the slightest.

"Do you want to go look in on his press conference?" Cliff asked her when she gave up in her attempt to feed LJ.

"Yeah. Wait, we can do that?" she asked and Cliff nodded, chuckling a little.

"Come on." He led them down to the bowels of the stadium then and stood just outside of the press room. Layla knew better than to go in, though she saw families standing at the back of the room. There were a few TVs playing what was being recorded outside and Layla simply watched that.

"Dominique, it was a great game you had today. You showed an overall great performance with the team, in your own finishes and moving the ball. Though you have great performances like this almost every game, was there anything that drove you?"

Layla knew that whoever asked that question was trying to get one specific response from Dominique. He chuckled before answering—he knew it too.

"Well, you know, uh, every game I always try to come out and do my best. But this was a special game, I have to admit. My son was watching me play for the first time, live. He was up in the booth, his mouth on the glass I think I saw at one point…" He paused for a chuckle and Layla smirked. LJ was pretty much trying to attach himself to the window, he wanted to get to his dad so badly. The press asked Dominique more about LJ than the game and after a while he had to ask them to ask about the game when questions started leaning toward Layla.

"He's good. Obviously used to the press," Cliff said thoughtfully.

Layla simply nodded, agreeing with him. His phone started to ring and he answered it quickly, walking away a few paces. Lucas saw his dad stepping off of "the hot seat" so to speak and started talking up a storm.

"Don't worry, he'll come out in a little bit," Layla told him.

"Layla, I just got some word that there's a problem at the prototype factory. I have to get over there," Cliff told her apologetically.

"Oh, okay then, yeah, go do what you have to do," she said understandingly.

"I'll email you the information about the office assistant job and who you should get into contact with," he said before backing away and Layla nodded, waving him off. She hoped everything was all right at that factory.

"Hey, how'd you guys get down here?" Dominique stepped out of the press room and LJ went right to him.

"Were we not supposed to be?" she asked and he laughed at her expression.

"Of course you can be, I was just joking. So where's Cliff?" he asked.

"He had to go and handle something with work. It sounded like an emergency."

"All right then, are you still up for dinner?"

Layla nodded and she glanced at LJ a little baffled that he wasn't hungry yet, probably still too excited.

"Yeah, definitely, I'm starved," she said and he wrapped an arm around her waist to lead them out to his car. Layla wondered briefly who had John, or if he went home.

"Did you let John know he was off for the night?" she asked him idly while getting LJ strapped in.

"Yes, I let John know," Dominique said.

And if Layla knew any better she'd say she heard some annoyance in his voice.

"What's wrong?" She chuckled and straightened from the backseat to face him.

"Nothing, I actually have a big franchise dinner coming up and I wanted you to go with me."

Layla briefly didn't know what to say.

"Isn't that… uh, that sounds important," she said hesitantly.

"It is an important event for the team and I want you there by my side," he said sincerely and without hesitation.

"Are you sure?" she asked, honestly a bit baffled that he was asking her to such an event.

"If I wasn't, I wouldn't have asked you," he said simply and cupped her face in his hands. "I think I've made a bad go at conveying my feelings properly…" he said sheepishly, then he bent down and pressed his lips against hers. The kiss was soft and measured, but he moved his lips against hers deliberately, his hands were at the small of her back and held her in place against his much larger body.

Layla broke the kiss before she could forget herself and become lost to him. They were both a bit out of breath and he was still holding her close.

"So, conveying your feelings?" she asked him with a smirk and he chuckled.

"I want you, and I want our family more than anything," he said, his green gaze never leaving hers.

A swell of emotion ballooned in her chest, most of it was joy, and Layla had a hard time responding.

"That sounds good," was all she was able to get out and he laughed at her.

"Good, so no more talking about John," he said, making her laugh.

They got into the car finally and Dominique drove to an intimate family restaurant near the house. Layla liked it because it wasn't too packed and also because it was Italian food, which she learned that she had a love for.

"So how have you been faring, getting to know your dad and all?" Dominique asked her once they were seated at a table. He had LJ in his arms and was feeding him a bottle.

"It's been really nice and easy, which is surprising to him more than me. He always thought that I'd have a hard time with reconciling how he left my mother and having to live without much money, but honestly there's nothing you can do to affect the past. So if you want to have a happy future, you just have to move on I guess," Layla said.

"Layla… you—you're one of the very best people I know. So many others just wouldn't have an outlook like you do," he said.

"My mom was a kind person and she taught me that there was no use in being callous or begrudging."

"But wouldn't people take kindness for weakness?" he asked her.

She thought about Isabelle briefly and shrugged.

"Yes, but there's a strength in it that most people underestimate. Being humble has its own rewards," she shrugged.

"I'm glad LJ has you as his mom," Dominique said, then added, "I'm glad I didn't have a child with Isabelle."

Layla snorted, wondering how *that* would have gone.

"If I may…?" He gave her a nod and she continued, "How'd you guys get together? Like, what was your draw to her?"

"When we first met and got together, she was just coming up as a great singer. She was a lot more humble. I thought she was different than other people of fame, but the bigger she got, the bigger her head got, and it took me until LJ to realize she wasn't going to change. She wasn't going to go back to the person I thought I knew."

Layla nodded thoughtfully to that.

They had a nice dinner. Really it felt more like a date than anything, especially when LJ fell asleep almost as soon as he was done eating. When they got home and put LJ to bed, Layla wondered if Dominique would stay or head to his house.

"Are you tired?" she asked him.

They were standing in the kitchen, sharing a hot chocolate.

"Not that tired, actually. Usually, I'm ready to dive into bed after a game," he said with a bit of surprise in his voice.

Layla glanced at the clock on the stove—it was pushing midnight.

"So when is the dinner?" she asked him.

"Tomorrow," he said with a big grin on his face.

"Seriously? What do you even wear to a franchise dinner? Do I have to dress up fancy?" she asked him, panicking only a little.

"Calm down, don't worry. I'll take care of you. All you have to do is go with everything," he said, rather suspiciously.

"So if someone shows up at the house to kidnap and murder me?"

Dominique laughed out loud, shaking his head.

"Trust me, that won't happen." He chuckled and then circled around the breakfast bar to pull Layla close. Every time she was in his arms, she got a little breathless. She couldn't help it, he was just that pretty. "I wouldn't let anything happen to you, or LJ," he vowed and simply kissed her.

Layla was very aware that it was late, and they were alone. Nothing would stop them from going further than a kiss… and she was right. The soft peck turned into a heated kiss, his tongue licking into her mouth and his lips moving against hers almost urgently. She let out a soft moan when he pulled her lip in between his teeth, biting down with the perfect amount of pressure.

Before she knew it, he had lifted her up, her legs hooked around his waist, and was walking her toward the stairs. She held on to his shoulders and broke the kiss, more to catch her breath than anything.

"Is this okay?" he asked her, his voice a little hoarse.

She simply nodded and he picked up the pace in getting to her bedroom, shutting the door behind them. He landed with her on the bed and quickly pulled off his shirt, her hands went to his strong chest and slid down his defined abdomen. She always used to kiss his chest when they were together before and had the urge to do so again. Only he captured her wrists in his hand and held them above her head. His lips went to her neck, which was one of the more sensitive parts of her body and he knew it. He slid his tongue just underneath her ear and her hips swiveled underneath him. She was getting way too warm and wanted to have less clothing on at the moment.

Dominique's lips slid to her collar and she moaned when he nibbled on the sensitive skin there. Her fingers tightened on his sides as his own slid underneath her sweater. He had her top off in one smooth motion and unhooked her bra, pulling it off in another. It took no time before he had her breasts cupped in his hands and his teeth on one of her nipples. She cried out, a mix of sensations speared down to her core. Her breasts were usually sensitive since she was pregnant with Lucas. Dominique teased her nipples with his teeth until her back was arched and she was breathless with the pleasure coursing through her. She knew her panties were soaked even before he slid his fingers beneath her waist band. They grazed her cleft and he sucked in a breath between his teeth.

"I can't wait any longer. You're so wet," he whispered and practically tore his pants off, removing the rest of her clothes too when he was done.

He pressed his body against hers and she felt his hard and thick erection against her belly. She met his lips with hers for a passionate kiss as he nudged her legs a bit farther apart. She felt the head of his sex at her entrance and he slowly pushed inside. She moaned as he filled her up and her sex clenched around him tight, she knew it wouldn't take much before she climaxed. Dominique did that thing, made that sound that was half whimper, half groan that Layla loved to hear. Like she was giving him exactly what he needed.

She held onto his arms, readying for his usually hard and fast stroke, but he was gentle with her. His gaze never left hers as he moved his hips slowly against hers, pushing deep and touching the very heart of her. Her limbs were all liquid and she felt as if she'd melt into nothing, her mind encased in a haze of pleasure. All she could do was hold onto him. Dominique pushed her over the edge again and again, until they were both spent. Even so, he still cleaned her up afterwards and Layla felt the tenderness between them like a tangible thing. She knew her heart was all kinds of on the line and a part of her was fearful of that still.

# *Chapter 8*

Come morning, Layla opened her eyes to an empty bed. She frowned and sat up, glancing around the room for signs of Dominique. His shoes were still on the floor, as well as his shirt. She got up and stretched, secretly loving the tightness in her belly, evidence of a night well spent with Dom. She freshened up a little and pulled on a pair of sweat pants and a jacket. She found Dominique downstairs, shirtless, holding LJ while fixing him a bottle.

"There you are," she said, her voice a little sleepy still.

"Good morning." He smiled at her and gestured to the coffee pot, filled with the dark deliciousness and waiting for her to pour a cup.

"Bless you," she said and went to give LJ a kiss before grabbing her coffee mug. She poured herself a cup and was about to add sugar when she realized Dominique was pouting at her. "What's wrong?" she asked, a small smile growing on her lips.

"What about me?" He puckered his lips and she giggled, but went over to give him a kiss good morning as well. "Much better," he said and she shook her head at him fondly.

"So for the dinner, I need you to be free by three this afternoon," Dom told her.

"When is the dinner?"

"At seven…"

"That's four hours for what exactly?" she asked him and he simply smirked at her.

"You'll see. John's going to pick you up at three, so be ready. I already called Nadia so she's good to watch LJ from then."

"So what are you doing today?" she asked him.

"Spending time with you, until three," he said with a chuckle and leaned over to kiss her again. LJ touched both of their faces and gave one sloppy kiss to first Layla then Dominique.

"He's the cutest baby ever," she sighed, smiling at LJ.

"I know. He is," Dominique said as if the fact were written in stone somewhere. Layla's phone chirped and she went to take it off the charger. She had the habit of leaving her phone to charge overnight in the kitchen. She saw Tony was calling and was quick to answer.

"Cousin!" she said happily.

"Hey Layla, guess what?" he answered just as happily.

"You're coming to visit?" she said, hoping for the best.

"Yep, this weekend. Only three days away," he said proudly. Layla had a bit of a girly moment as the excitement bubbled up in her chest.

"I can't wait! You can meet my dad and see LJ and oh, we can go to one of Dominique's games; it's going to be so much fun," she said, making him laugh as well as Dominique who was watching her bounce around uninhibited.

They made plans for the weekend and he told her his flight details. Right after she hung up with Tony, her dad called.

"Hey, Cliff," she answered, still upbeat from her conversation with Tony.

"Hey, Layla, you sound pretty happy," he said with a chuckle and she told him that Tony was visiting for the weekend.

"So how was everything with the prototype lab?" she asked him.

"There was a small fire, but it was contained—no lasting damage. But it means my stay here will be longer."

Layla was happy to hear that, she was growing really fond of Cliff.

"Anyway I wanted to call to see if you got my e-mail. The guys at the office there are going to need that position filled soon. They're waiting for your call," he told her and she promised she'd follow up with the job right away. She grabbed her coffee cup and went upstairs to the loft to use the computer. About thirty minutes later, after talking to a guy named Todd, she had a job and was set to start on Monday instead of right away since everyone in the office was busy at the prototype lab seeing what went wrong with the new processor they'd been conceptualizing for years.

"Guess what?" Layla said as she went back downstairs to join her guys in the kitchen. "I finally got a job," she announced.

"That's great! When do you start?"

"Monday, which is perfect," she said happily.

Layla couldn't help but mark the day as a really good one. It was starting out so well.

"Things are finally in place." He smiled at her and she took a deep breath.

"Yeah... they are."

For the first time in a very long time, Layla was truly hopeful for the future.

\*\*\*

"Dominique...you've done too much," Layla said as she gazed down at the beautiful dress he bought for her. She was already pampered after spending some time at the spa, getting her nails and toes done, as well as her hair and even makeup. She felt sort of like a princess. Then, to top it all off, he went and bought her a simple, yet elegant and sexy, dinner dress along with gorgeous silver heels with red bottoms. It was a long, cream-colored sheath dress. It had one long lace sleeve and was sleeveless across the other side. There was a slit for her leg that went pretty high up, too.

"I know you'll look perfect in it," he said, eager for her to get dressed.

She took the clothes and went into his huge walk-in closet to get dressed. Luckily, the zipper was on the side so she didn't need any help getting into the dress. When she slid her feet into the shoes, she was surprised at how comfortable they were. Appraising herself in the mirror, she had to say, she looked good. Her hair was blow-dried straight and pinned to fall over her shoulder. She had forgotten how long her hair was until then. She was as ready as she'd ever be and stepped out to find Dominique, who was still waiting in the bedroom dressed in his tux, his hair gelled back, looking as if he belonged in an Armani ad.

He glanced at her and did a double-take, his jaw going a bit slack. She chuckled and rolled her eyes at him.

"Really Dom?" she said and he simply nodded his head.

"You look amazing… beyond amazing. I'm reconsidering taking you out and having other men look at you," he said, making her really laugh then.

"It's too late to back out anyhow, you said this dinner was important, so come on," she said and made to leave the bedroom, but he stepped into her path and cupped her face in his hands.

"I bet they didn't even put a lot of makeup on you," he breathed before giving her the lightest of kisses and causing goose bumps to race across her skin.

"They didn't actually… I didn't want too much caked on," she said almost sheepishly.

Dominique closed his eyes briefly and then kissed her again before he took her hand, placing it on his arm to escort her like a proper gentleman. They went downstairs to the waiting car. LJ was at Layla's house with Nadia, who was eager to start working for them. She'd come in handy a lot more when Layla started working and going to school, though she felt a little weird about being so busy when LJ was still so young. She didn't want to miss out on the big things.

"Where'd you go?" Dominique touched Layla's chin to get her attention.

He had rented a car for the night so that he wouldn't have to drive. She had been gazing out of the window while he held her hand in his lap.

"I was just thinking about LJ. How I won't be spending as much time with him anymore… I don't want to miss anything."

"We won't, don't worry. We'll still get to see him every day. He won't forget that we're his parents," Dominique assured her and she nodded.

"So… is everyone who's remotely part of the team going to be at the dinner?"

"Yeah, it's a whole big thing. There are a couple per year, one at the beginning of the season, another at the end."

"There's going to be press there," Layla said, more wanting to confirm the fact more than ask.

"Yeah, but no tabloid paparazzi. It should all be fine; just stick by my side," he said and she nodded again, feeling a little nervous.

It was a bit of a drive to the hotel where the dinner was being had. Then, when the car pulled up to the curb, their doors were opened by valet and Layla was met with a red carpet that was kept clear of fans and some cameras by security. Dominique was quick to her side, looping her arm through his. She tried not to get overwhelmed and simply followed his lead, smiling, and walking along. Thankfully, he didn't make any stops along the way to sign autographs or take pictures with his fans. When they made it to the lobby, Layla let out a small breath of relief.

"That was… crazy," she said in a low voice and Dominique chuckled.

"It wasn't that bad," he assured her, which only had Layla's eyes widening.

They made their way to the hotel's main ballroom. Outside the entrance was where pictures were being taken of players, franchise members, and those associated with them. When it came time for Dominique to step forward with Layla, more pictures were taken, some photographers giving them directions to take pictures together, apart, smile more, smile less. By the time she and

Dominique were able to walk inside, she felt she may be blind in one eye and little bit like she had vertigo.

The night didn't slow down, though. Once they were inside, it was a whirlwind of being introduced to people and making small talk, all while trying not to act as if she was *way* out of her depth. Afterwards, when dinner actually started, there were a few speeches given, hoping for another season to go all the way, talking about the team, the players, the coaches and so on. After dinner and dessert, a DJ came out and some people stayed to make a party of the dinner, but thankfully, Dominique pulled Layla toward the exit after all was said and done.

"That wasn't so bad, right? Everyone seemed to like you, they like you a lot better than Isabelle—I could tell." He laughed to himself while they waited for an elevator.

"Well it was… it was a little overwhelming, but not bad," she agreed. "And are you sure your teammates liked me?" she asked him.

"Yes, they do trust me. Isabelle never likes to meet new people. She's secretly socially awkward. So they all assumed she was a bitch to be honest."

"Wow…" Layla said slowly, not knowing how to really respond to that.

"Yeah, but let's not talk about her. Was it okay for you that I had introduced you as, well, simply Layla?"

"Honestly, I didn't really notice, but Layla is my name so, I guess so?" she answered, not really catching his drift.

"I mean, as in not in anything specific to me," he said and Layla finally got it.

They had reached the car by then and only just began moving.

"Um…" was her only response. She supposed that after the night they had before and all, that she'd be more than simply "Layla" to him.

"I only did it so you wouldn't be uncomfortable. We haven't exactly had 'that talk' yet," he quickly explained. "I don't want to push you or make you feel cornered in case you don't, I don't know, feel for me," he added.

"Of course I do, Dominique, or else we wouldn't… None of what happened the past twenty-four hours would have happened," she said.

"Did you have feelings for me… when we were first together?" he asked her.

Layla wouldn't answer the question though; she didn't want to put herself out there so much.

"I think I want a nightcap when I get home," she sighed to herself, but Dominique heard her and laughed.

"Why don't we share one?" he asked, humor in his eyes. She smirked at him, nodding.

"Sounds like a good play, Captain," she teased and he chuckled.

The rest of the ride was spent in relative quiet, all the while Layla felt the spark between them growing stronger. She knew exactly what sort of nightcap she was in for with him. When they got to Layla's house, Nadia filled them in on her night with LJ who was a good boy all night and sleeping in his room. After she left, Layla went to check on him. He was indeed fast asleep in his crib and she gave him a kiss on his cheek. Dominique followed her into the room to do the same, then he practically hauled her straight to the bedroom.

"You know, Dominique, I'm going to end up pregnant again," Layla said and he actually laughed.

"You don't want another baby?" he asked her, pulling her down onto the bed with him, they were both still fully clothed. His hand on her calf and slowly making its way north.

"Well, I don't know. Maybe yeah, when I'm *married* and doing things the right way," she said pointedly, hoping to throw him off a bit.

It had the opposite effect though; he simply continued to push her dress up while his other hand traveled to her inner thighs.

199

"So tell me something, then. Would you rather I ruin the bed sheets? Would you rather I finished on your skin?"

Layla's mouth opened and closed. She was at a loss for words and quickly losing the battle there.

"Dominique… are you saying…?"

He shut her up with a kiss and kept her unable to speak for the rest of the night.

Come morning, she was woken up by what felt like soft flower petals touching her nose. She opened her eyes and saw Dominique holding a single red rose right in front of her face. She smiled and took it from him, sitting up in the process.

"Good morning." He smiled at her and pulled the blanket up to cover her naked hips.

"Morning…" she said and then discovered a trail of rose petals leading into the bathroom.

"Thought you'd like a nice bath before LJ woke," he said. "With me," he added with a boyish grin.

"That sounds heavenly, actually," she said, inflating his smile even more. She got up and he carried her into the bathroom. "Oh my goodness, you set this all up yourself?" she gasped when she saw the candles and bath drawn in the tub along with more rose petals floating in the water.

"Yes, I am a romantic," he said proudly and quickly slid out of his gym shorts to get into the water with Layla.

The bath was actually perfect, there was the right amount of bath salts. She knew he definitely had practice in drawing baths.

"Do you usually draw baths for yourself after practice?" she asked him and he laughed, nodding a little as if he was embarrassed. "Hey, I'm not complaining." She giggled.

"I have practice today. Wish I didn't." He sighed as he lowered into the tub across from her.

"What time is it?" she asked, realizing the sun hadn't even fully risen into the sky.

"Five." He grinned at her sheepishly and her eyes widened. She ended up laughing and he did, too. "You know… sometimes I have trouble thinking you're real," he said and she felt his toes tickling her legs.

"How come?" She laughed, tilting her head to run water through her hair, curling it up.

"Because you're so… *real*," he said, making no sense to Layla whatsoever. "You're not like the women I've gotten used to. You're kind and genuine and… normal." He laughed. "It's like when I met you, you had this calm around you, even in a crowd full of crazy fans. Whenever I'm with you I just feel… grounded," he said, a small contented sigh leaving his lips. "And I need that so much," he admitted.

Layla didn't know what to say, she wasn't sure she *could* say anything.

"Here I thought you mostly liked me because of LJ," she said with a short chuckle.

"I 'like' you even more because of him," he said sincerely.

"It's stuff like that that's going to ruin me, Dominique."

"Good, I don't want anyone else having you," he smirked.

"You turned out to be exactly what I hoped for, you know," she offered slowly.

"How so?" he asked, smiling at Layla charmingly.

"I thought you'd be a fairytale for me, distract me from the reality that was my life, but also, I don't know, feel the same way about me, too," she said with a small smile.

"I did that!" he said happily, as if he aced a test he was really hoping to pass.

Layla giggled at his pleased expression. They talked more, mostly about little things or silly things. They were both prunes by the time LJ woke up, making noise through the baby monitor.

"Hey, little man," Dominique said as he went to scoop LJ out of the crib.

Lucas smiled wide seeing his dad, babbling happily. They were about to go down to the kitchen for breakfast when the doorbell rang. Layla glanced at the clock and saw it was just barely seven in the morning.

"I don't think my dad would come by unannounced."

Dominique followed her down and she checked her phone, but saw no calls or texts from her dad.

"I'll check to see who it is," Dominique said, passing LJ to her.

She was in nothing but a robe, meanwhile Dominique was going to the door in nothing but a pair of his team breakaway pants. She got out one of LJ's bottles and got ready to warm it up while putting on a pot of coffee.

"What are you doing here? Why…?"

Layla glanced over her shoulder, in the direction of the foyer, though she couldn't see anything, curious as to who it was. Most importantly, why Dominique rose his voice as soon as he opened the door.

"I just need to talk to you, and you weren't home…" Layla froze when she heard Isabelle's voice

"You have no right to be here," he said angrily.

Layla started to rub LJ's back before he could pick up on what was going on and start crying.

"Will you just hear me out?" she said, as impassioned as Layla's ever heard her.

"What else is there to hear, Isabelle?" he asked her, still highly upset.

"I just… I want to fix things and you're not answering my calls. You won't see me. I didn't know what else to do."

"Isabelle, I told you that things are over between us," he said, trying to measure his tone.

"How can you just *end* things on your own after being together so long? Because of what? Layla?"

Contempt edged into her voice and Layla tried not to breathe so she could catch Dominique's next words.

"Isabelle, you and I *both* know that things weren't good between us. That the engagement was nothing, just a smoke screen. I'm happy with Layla and I'm happy with our family. Please just learn to let go so you can be happy, too," he said in a lower voice.

"Just… 'learn to *let go?*' Are you serious with that bullshit?!" she yelled. "You're an asshole, Dominique. It won't be long before she realizes it and leaves you!"

With that, the door opened and slammed shut. LJ had a start and began to cry, so Layla bounced him in her arms to try and calm him down.

"I'm sorry, Layla, I…" Dominique came into the kitchen, at a loss for words.

"It's all right, Dom, don't apologize," she said and smiled at him.

He went right over to her and gave her a hard kiss, then he took LJ and whispered to him, trying to soothe him. She made breakfast for everyone. Omelets for her and Dom and a bottle for LJ.

"These are some of the best eggs I've ever eaten," Dominique said with a full mouth.

"Please, I'm sure you've had a bunch of good omelets before." Layla laughed.

"They weren't made with *your* hands." He smiled at her, making her laugh all over again.

"You have no time to flatter the chef. You have work today," she reminded him.

"You're coming to the game tonight, right?"

"Yes and I'm bringing John..." she said slowly.

Dominique actually growled.

"Well, why don't you sit in floor seats tonight then?" he suggested, though it sounded less like a suggestion and more like an order.

She quirked a brow at him and he huffed.

"Why do you have to have guy friends?" he pouted.

"Because sometimes friendships happen Dominique," she said, wondering if he was really serious.

"Fine, bring John," he mumbled and went back to his omelet.

"Dominique, no one's going to steal me away. Trust me," she assured him.

"I'm not trying to be a douche or anything I just... I really want you," he said, touching Layla's heart yet again that morning.

What's more is that she realized he was a bit insecure. Why? She had next to no clue. She told him that he pretty much had her already. They finished eating in relative silence and Layla started to burp Lucas as Dominique got ready to head to practice.

"I'll see you tonight, then," he said when she walked him to the door.

"Yeah, see you tonight," she said and he gave her a hard kiss before leaving.

"Guess it's just you and me," she told LJ who smiled at her, hugging her neck. She was pretty tired from the night before, especially after being woken up at five in the morning. So she spent the rest of the morning simply relaxing with LJ.

When the time came around to head to the stadium, John showed up at Layla's.

"Hey, ready to go?" he asked, some excitement in his eyes.

"Yeah, definitely. Let me just get LJ's bag," she said, inviting John inside. Lucas' bag was with his stroller, so she simply lowered him inside and soon they were on their way. Before entering the stadium, Layla pulled out Lucas' fancy headphones to cancel out the noise of the crowd. He looked too cute, but also silly with them on. Then the way he was gazing at Layla, as if she attached some alien substance to his head and didn't like it at all. She kissed him on the mouth then followed John through the parking garage to the elevators. After getting their tickets and armbands for clearance, they found their seats right next to the Horns bench. The teams were out on the court, warming up. Dominique glanced over at the bench and spotted them. He waved, sending them a huge grin. Layla smiled in return and LJ reached for him, squirming in Layla's lap. She knew he wouldn't have a good time during that game.

"Can I ask you something?" John said with a mischievous smirk and she nodded, a slow smile growing on her lips. "Do you know what position he plays?" he gestured toward Dominique and Layla burst into laughter.

"Shoot... I don't. That's really bad isn't it?" she said, laughing all over again.

"It is, yeah, kinda." He laughed. Layla glanced up, only to find Dominique walking purposefully toward them. She wasn't sure if they were allowed to walk off the court during shoot out.

"Are you allowed...?"

"The bench is here, convenient right?" he smirked, though it didn't reach his eyes. Something was bothering him.

"Hey, what position do you play?" She leaned toward him to whisper and he stared at her blankly for a moment before he chuckled, then started laughing.

"Shooting guard. Sometimes I go in as a forward." He smirked.

"Oh, okay then, go ahead, don't get in trouble," she hissed and he flashed her a mischievous grin that did reach his eyes then.

Layla noticed one of his coaches staring him down. H

e ordered Dominique back on the court when their eyes met. It was all business in the stadium, no room for distraction. Layla was still embarrassed; she didn't even know what position he played. She shook her head at herself and John chuckled at her, patting her shoulder in support.

"Let's keep this between us okay?" she whispered and he gave her a nod and winked at her.

"Mum's the word," he said.

When the game started, Layla tried to enjoy it and watch Dominique play as if it were second nature, which for him, it was. But Lucas was having a bad time and Layla seemed to keep missing every great play and major basket. She got LJ settled enough to watch the fourth quarter. Surprisingly, Chicago was tied with Miami. The Horns had the ball and Dominique was crossing up every defender that got in his way. He drove to the basket and made a perfect layup, drawing a foul and causing the stadium to erupt. Layla tried to dampen her reaction. She wanted to be standing and cheering, but LJ still had a sour face as he watched the court. After Dominique's free throw, which he made effortlessly, they were five points in the lead with two minutes to go.

Miami had the ball, but the player handling it was all over the place with his dribbles, and it was as if no one from Chicago was guarding him, they were all trying to protect the point. Before Layla knew it, she was standing up with LJ and yelling at Dominique.

"He's got butter fingers, Dom! Steal the ball!" she shouted, and he actually heard her.

He barely glanced her way, but she caught his wink. Lighting quick, he ran up to the one with the ball and his hand shot out, perfectly stealing the ball. He ran all the way down the court and performed the flashiest Michael Jordan dunk. The stadium was as loud as Layla had ever heard it. For a moment she wished she had her own noise-canceling headphones. For the last minute and few seconds, Chicago played defense and won by four points. When Dominique came back to the bench, she gave him a high five and he kissed LJ on the head. Lucas definitely wanted his dad, reaching for him when Dominique made to go give an interview.

"Don't worry, you'll see him soon," she murmured to Lucas.

She needed to feed him soon or else he'd be inconsolable. She followed John out to the quieter hallway outside of the locker rooms and press room. Layla sat with Lucas on a nearby bench and tested to see if he'd drink room temperature milk. He did, and with vigor.

"That was a great game. I can't believe Dom heard you at the end." John chuckled.

"I know, my voice is kind of scratchy because of that." She laughed with him.

"Excuse me, miss?" Layla glanced up to see someone with a press badge walking toward her. "Hi, I'm with the *Sentinel*, would it be all right if I get a quick statement from you? On your advice for Dom out there on the court?" he asked nicely with a slightly nervous, but good-natured chuckle. Layla wasn't sure if she should be "giving statements."

"Uh… I'm not sure," she said slowly.

"Well, it's just so we have a bit of character to Dominique's performance tonight. After having game after game of him just being the perfect player, our readers want to have an interesting tidbit, just to switch it up," he explained.

"Well, I only noticed that the player with the ball was sort of all over the place with his dribbling. Then it seemed like none of the Chicago players wanted to go after him, they probably didn't want to risk fouling. But I knew Dom could steal the ball, so I yelled at him," she said with a small shrug and the reporter jotted what she said down, a small smile on his lips.

"Thank you, miss, and just to double check your name is Layla Anderson?" he asked and she nodded.

"Layla…" Dominique's voice had everyone's attention turning to him. He was walking swiftly toward her. "You're really trying to get something from her while she's feeding our son?" Dominique spoke to the reporter in annoyance.

"Calm down, Dom, he wasn't being any sort of way. He's nice," she said, defending the poor guy who suddenly looked wide-eyed and beyond nervous.

"Why don't you go in the press room with the rest of them?" Dominique pointed and the reporter mumbled some apology and thanks rolled into one before scurrying away. Upon seeing his dad, LJ reached up and he wasn't even done with his bottle.

"He's missed you today," Layla said, handing LJ over with his bottle. "And you didn't have to be so mean," she lightly chastised him and he snorted.

"Once the press sees that you're approachable, they'll all swarm to get something out of you. There's a time and place, plus they have no reason approaching you like this."

He glanced at John, who was standing to the side, looking anywhere but at Dominique. Thankfully, Dom spared him and simply deflated a little with a sigh.

"Is it okay if I take him in there with me?"

Layla nodded, sending LJ in with Dom.

"So is our bet honored?" Layla asked John who nodded with a chuckle.

"Yeah, seeing you yell at Dom like that was priceless." He laughed.

She punched him in the arm, and of course, the ex-army man hardly budged. In fact, Layla was sure she tickled him because he only laughed harder. Layla's attention turned to the TV screens airing the press conference going on then. Dom was up at the table holding LJ who was almost done with his bottle. Everyone was commending him on his performance and mostly asking questions about him seeming distracted by LJ and Layla sitting courtside as well as Layla's brief coaching stunt and calling another star player on Miami's team "butter fingers." Layla had no idea who were the big names in basketball yet. She only knew a few. She started to feel embarrassed for her outburst then.

"Looks like everyone liked your stunt," John snickered and she had the urge to hit him again.

"Would you shut up?" She couldn't help smile. Once the press conference was over, Dominique came out with a groggy LJ.

"That's done. Are you up for dinner?" he asked her, still ignoring the fact that John was standing there.

"Sure, but let's cook at home or something—LJ is beat," she said. Layla glanced at John then. "See you later?"

"Yeah, thanks for the game," he said, and they said a quick goodbye before parting ways.

"So when does Tony get in tomorrow?" Dominique asked as they made their way to his car.

"Nine in the morning, so I actually need a little sleep tonight," she said and Dom simply snorted.

"Sure, sleep, yeah," he said with a mischievous smile.

Layla glanced down at LJ—he was sleeping in his stroller, looking cute as ever.

"His hair is getting longer," she noticed. His curls were fuller and starting to frame his face just a little. Dominique got him into his car seat and soon they were on the way to her house.

"You have the day off tomorrow?" she asked him idly, figuring they could all do something with Tony the next day.

"Yeah, what do you think Tony will be up for?"

"I'm not sure…" she murmured, contemplative.

They got home pretty quickly after that. Layla put LJ to bed. She wandered out to the hallway, looking for Dominique and found him in her bedroom. He was stretched out at the foot of the bed, watching TV.

"Oh my God… they have that on camera?" Layla said, horrified, as she watched the clip of her getting up with LJ at the game and yelling at Dom to steal the ball.

Dominique laughed and changed the channel from ESPN.

"It was funny, more so because you called an all-star player 'butter fingers.'" He snickered and she hopped on the bed to grab a pillow and hit him with it. He grabbed her around the waist and easily pinned her down to the bed, a smug smile on his face. "I win," he said and she stuck her tongue out at him.

He lowered his head and sealed his mouth over hers. His tongue slipped into her mouth as he lowered some more of his weight onto her. Layla squirmed underneath him and slid her hands beneath his sweater, splaying them on his lower back.

He broke the kiss to press his lips just underneath Layla's ear and she shivered, pulling his hips down flush with hers. She could already feel how good it would be to have him inside of her and she was impatient for it. Dominique pulled her up to unbutton her sweater and push it off her shoulders, followed by unhooking her bra. She pushed her fingers through his hair, loving the feel of his silky curls around her fingers. He kissed her again, softly, as his arms encircled her waist.

"Can you tell me something?" he murmured against her lips before kissing her neck.

"What?" she replied distractedly, her voice breathless as she pushed his sweater off over his head.

"Do you love me?"

The question caught her completely off guard. She floundered a bit, her mouth opening and closing when words should be coming out. His green eyes were on hers, expectant and waiting.

"Yes… I do love you," she said honestly.

Dominique's eyes widened as if he expected her to answer differently, but how could she?

"Thank God," he breathed and got up, pulling her to the edge of the bed to get her bottoms off as well as his.

Layla still couldn't fathom his seeming insecurity in her feelings for him. They did have that talk the day before. Dominique gently pushed Layla down onto the bed and nudged her legs apart. He kissed her bellybutton and trailed kisses down to her cleft. Layla's core clenched in anticipation and heat coursed through her veins. Her breathing became erratic when his tongue slid against her clit. He slid one finger into her sex and she moaned, arching against his mouth. Her hands went to her aching nipples as Dominique was sending wave after wave of electric sensations through her. She felt, rather than heard, him growl and it only added to her pleasure. Dominique kept at it, not letting up with his mouth or fingers. Layla was a second away from climax when he suddenly stopped. She cried out in dismay and he actually chuckled at her.

"I always know when you're close…" he said hoarsely.

"Dominique…" she said in a needy voice.

He kissed her chest, moving her hands out of the way so that he could suck a nipple into his mouth. She shook and trembled underneath him, teetering on the edge in an almost painful height of pleasure. She felt the head of his sex at her entrance. As soon as he pushed fully inside, Layla went flying into climax. Dominique thrust into her hard and fast, not letting up even as another orgasm hit her.

Five orgasms later, Layla felt as if she was one with the mattress underneath her. She couldn't move even if she wanted to.

"I feel like I've been given the best internal massage ever," she said, her voice sounded a little drunk even to her ears.

Dominique laughed at her and she turned her head toward him, smiling.

"Should we order some pizza?" he asked her as he got up. She nodded, though she felt more like sleeping than eating pizza. Her eyelids drooped a bit, but then she woke some when Dominique picked her up, taking her to the bathroom for a shower. He took very good care of her, washing every inch of her it seemed. After Dominique's pizza got there, they cuddled on the couch downstairs, watching a movie, until Layla dozed off and she felt him carrying her off to bed.

# *Chapter 9*

Layla woke up in degrees. She knew Dominique and LJ were next to her as she felt his warmth and could hear Lucas babbling away.

"Finally awake. Look at you, sleepy head." She smiled as she opened her eyes. Dominique was all dressed as well as Lucas. "I just sent a car to pick Tony up. He should be here in about an hour."

"How long have you been awake?" she asked groggily.

"Like, an hour. LJ and I had enough time to go out and bring back some breakfast."

Dom let Layla get ready for the day. When she walked out to the kitchen, he had a cup of coffee waiting for her.

"You two are my saviors, thank you." She kissed both LJ and Dominique on the cheek and sat at the breakfast bar with her coffee. She texted Tony to see if he was on the way to her house or still at the airport. Instead of replying through text, he called her back.

"Hey, where are you?" she answered.

"I just got in the car Dom sent. I wanted to see if you'd like to visit Mom and Aunt Lori before we do anything?"

Layla felt a small pang in her chest. She and Tony usually visited their mothers' graves every other month. She hadn't been to her mother's grave since she found out she was pregnant with Lucas. The cemetery was in a rougher part of the South Side.

"Of course, yeah we can do that," she said, her voice already wavering.

She had come to terms with the fact that her mom was gone a long time ago, but whenever she even thought about visiting her, Layla always got choked up, memories bombarding her left and right.

"You okay?" Dominique asked her as she ended the call.

"Yeah, it's just that Tony wants to visit our moms' graves today for a little bit, before we do anything."

"Oh... do you want us to come with you?" he asked gently.

"No, no, the graveyard they're in is in a bad part of town..." she said hurriedly.

"Then you guys will take John," he said sternly. Layla didn't argue. She didn't want him to end up sending Green Berets in with them. "Do you visit your mother often?" he asked her as she mostly poked at her omelet and potatoes.

"Every month or two... I usually go with Tony." She wondered briefly if she should call Cliff to go along with them, but figured she could go with him alone on another occasion.

"Do you miss her a lot?"

"I do miss her, but it all hits me hard whenever we go visit the grave. I just feel her so strongly there," she said sadly.

"That's good though, sometimes you need that," he told her and cupped her jaw, lifting her head just in time to receive his kiss.

LJ leaned forward to press his mouth to her cheek as well. Layla giggled, an intense feeling of melancholy saturating her chest. She wished her mom was there to see how great her family was, though Layla was sure she was watching from somewhere up above.

"I love you both," she said softly and Dominique rubbed her back reassuringly.

"We love you, too," he said sincerely.

She looked at him then, aware he hasn't exactly said "I love you," but in a way, it was just as well for Layla. After that, Dominique lightened the mood by telling her jokes about his team and such.

"Oh! So for Christmas, do you plan on going to California, or have you discussed that with your dad yet?" Dom asked her.

"He's actually thinking about staying through until New Year's," she said. "Why?"

"Because my mom and uncle are coming from France and my father's family want to formally meet you. The whole family will be here," he said with an almost-sheepish smile.

"Of course, yeah, I'll be here to spend time with your family," she said, actually feeling a little nervous at the prospect of meeting Dominique's mom.

"It will be a whole shebang, I must warn you," he chuckled.

"That sounds nice, actually. I like the idea of LJ having a big family, you know?"

He nodded and was about to say something else when the doorbell rang.

"He's here!"

Layla got instantly excited; she missed Tony so much. She ran to open the door and there he was. The Tony she loved: healthy, happy, and handsome.

"Layla!" he said happily and caught her as she launched into him for a hug. She hugged him tight and he did the same.

"Are we going to let him get in the door?" Dominique chuckled and she finally let him go so he could step inside. Tony greeted Dominique with one of the universal guy handshakes and a one-armed hug. Layla was almost surprised to see that John was Tony's driver.

"Hey, John." She smiled at him and he gave her a quick greeting, getting Tony's things in the door.

Layla paused briefly, wondering why John was so professional all of a sudden. She glanced at Dominique, wondering if he said anything he shouldn't have. Once Tony was past the foyer, he found LJ bouncing in his little stationary bouncer.

"There's the little man!" Tony said and LJ looked at him, as if he were trying to place him from somewhere. Then he gave the biggest smile, and if he could walk, Layla knew he'd be running toward Tony.

"He missed his uncle," Layla said, the scene so heartwarming she felt she could get teary.

"Man, he grew so much," Tony said and Layla nodded.

"Yeah, he's getting tall. Soon he'll be walking and... I can't even get into it," she said. Everyone always used the phrase, "they grow so fast." Well it was the absolute truth and Lucas wasn't even one yet.

"So did you eat? Want some coffee or something?" Layla offered.

"Oh yeah, I ate, don't worry about me. Though coffee would be good. It's freezing out there."

"Maryland weather done made you soft, huh?" she teased him.

"They just don't have the cold winds like we do," he said.

"So Tony, after you and Layla get back from the South Side, I was thinking we could go out on the town, find something to do," Dominique said.

"Yeah definitely, I'm down for anything," he said and put LJ back in his little play area off the kitchen. He looked at Layla then, expectantly.

"If you want to go now, I'll just go and put on some boots," she said and he nodded. She hurried upstairs to get a jacket and shoes, that feeling of melancholy rippling over her once again. "Okay, I'm ready," she said as she walked back downstairs.

Before they left with John, Dominique gave her a soft kiss on the lips and she could see the silent support in his gaze. She really did love him. Take away the basketball and Dominique would still be a good man.

"Have you visited their graves since I've been gone?" he asked her once they were in the car and moving.

"No, so much has happened that I… I sort of forgot about our tradition," she said and he shrugged a little.

"You know, it's okay to go a little longer and longer between visits. Living like they wanted us to live, being successful is paying tribute in itself. As long as we never forget them, never forget where we came from."

Layla nodded, what he said was absolutely right. But she felt she'd need the visits at least once every couple of months still. Living like Dominique does and Cliff, it can make a person forget what it was like to have such a humble upbringing. Where if you were fed, had a roof over your head, and clothes on your back everything was all right.

The closer they got to Englewood, the more Layla remembered her mom and her life there. She couldn't believe the diner was being turned into an IHOP, but things change. Hell, she changed.

"Do you think mom would've liked for me to... to have done a one-eighty lifestyle change like this?" she asked Tony suddenly.

"I think she's happy for you, as long as you stay true, you know? Stay the Layla I grew up with," he said and placed a comforting hand on her knee.

After stopping to get some flowers, they pulled into the graveyard and John parked on the road near their mothers' plots. Overhead, the clouds were thick in the sky, but Layla didn't see any rainclouds. She wondered if they'd be getting snow early again that year.

"Come on," Tony said, urging her out of the car.

John got out and stood by the car, giving them privacy, but also keeping an eye out. The graveyard was situated right in the middle of where most gang-related homicides and activity happened. It was neutral ground, but still. If opposing gangs spotted one another, no one hesitated to shoot. They found the two matching gravestones. Modest and simple, because that's all Layla and Tony could afford at the time. Layla's mom's said "Here lies Lorietta

223

Morrison, Mother & Sister." Tony's mom's read "Here lies Tasha Morrison, Mother & Sister." Seeing that always brought Layla to tears. Especially as her mother's grave should also say "Grandmother." She knelt down and wiped some water and frost off of the stone. Afterward, she arranged the flowers on top of the grave and simply sat there. Her mother's presence suddenly a real thing next to her.

"I'm sure you know, but I thought I'd tell you that you have a little grandson. His name's Lucas. He looks just like his dad, but sometimes he reminds me of you. He's just so happy all the time and, um, I met my dad. I know you had your issues with him, but he's changed and he's trying to do the right thing by me now. He's a great grandpa as well. He was devastated that you died. But I hope that you can forgive him."

Layla took a deep breath and glanced over at Tony who always stood next to Aunt Tasha's grave. After putting down the flowers, he'd talk to his mom in a low voice, just like Layla. Something flashed, sort of like lightning, in Layla's peripheral vision. She glanced around, but only saw one other person several yards away, they were standing over a grave, head down, shoulder's slumped, his hands in his pockets. She took another deep breath and stood up.

"Love you, Mom…" she said in a soft voice and took a step back to rub Tony's shoulder. He was almost smiling, a thoughtful expression on his face.

"Ready to go?" he asked he after a moment and she nodded.

"Yeah, I'm ready."

"Um… excuse me?"

Layla glanced over to see the man who she looked at earlier. He was walking toward them and seemed a bit tentative. The closer he got, the more Layla felt like she knew him.

"I don't know if you remember me, but I'm your neighbor. From Park Building?"

"That's right! Trevor, right?" she said and he nodded, a small smile on his lips. Trevor was a quiet neighbor. She'd see him when picking up mail or if they got home at the same time, making small talk and such.

"Yep, that's me. How've you been? How's that little baby of yours?"

Layla filled him in, somewhat, on how she was doing. She learned that Trevor actually moved as well, as the building they used to live in was about to be knocked down, a new one to be built in its place. After their brief conversation, they went their separate ways, Layla joining Tony and John at the car. Soon they were heading back to Layla's place. She always felt strangely lighter after visiting her mom, more at ease.

"So what do you and Dom have in mind for the day?" Tony asked and she shrugged.

"I don't know, I think we're just going to wing it," she said and he grinned.

"Sounds like we should visit another skyscraper," he said mischievously and she gave him a warning glare, which he laughed at of course.

"*You* can risk your life looking out on the top of those sky scrapers, but I'll stay right on level ground thank you very much."

Tony laughed at her again. When they got home, Dominique and LJ were ready to go out.

"So I planned the perfect day for us…" He went on to tell them how he set up a tour of one of Chicago's museums for them, which Tony was excited about because he secretly loved art. After that they'd grab lunch then get ready to catch a show at the Oriental Theater and have a fancy dinner out.

"So how was it? Visiting your mom?" Dominique asked while they were on the way to the museum. He brought his Mercedes SUV so everyone could fit in one car.

"It was nice. I caught her up on things and felt her there with me…" Layla said softly, just so he could hear her. Tony was in the back with LJ, making him laugh. Lucas was developing such a goofy little laugh, too; they were really entertaining each other back there.

"You know, I could go with you whenever you want to go, when Tony's not here," he said and slipped his hand around hers.

"I'd like that," she said and glanced at him with a smile.

When they got to the Art Institute they were met by the tour guide who was eager to lead them around the different exhibits they currently had up. While Tony, Layla, and Dominique enjoyed the tour, LJ was practically falling asleep in his stroller. They had lunch at a popular restaurant known for great street cuisine. Dominique hardly had time to eat his food though as people kept going up to him to take pictures. He actually had to eat in the car while Layla drove back to her place. She was actually a little nervous getting behind the wheel. Though she did have a license, she hadn't driven since she got it at sixteen. When they got home, they took it easy for a little bit then got ready for the show. Layla dressed LJ up in a little tux and Dominique took maybe a hundred pictures of him because he looked so cute.

They all got pretty fancy for the play. It was on the Broadway circuit and visiting only a few cities before going overseas. Layla had heard good things about it and wondered how similar it would be to the original *Lion King* movie.

"Are you ready yet, Layla? We have to get going," Dominique called up to her.

She had been fussing with her hair, trying to style it into a nice bun, but finally got it to do what she wanted.

"I'm coming, I'm coming," she said and grabbed her clutch before going to join the guys downstairs.

"Must you look so good?" Dominique said when Layla joined them in the foyer.

"What do you mean?" She chuckled and he sighed.

"I mean you look too gorgeous to step foot out of the house. I think we may need to put a bag over your head," he said, making Tony laugh.

"Oh stop," she said, though she smiled.

Dominique pulled her in for a kiss and Tony groaned.

"Please, can we go before I get sick?" he teased.

They filed out to the car and were on their way. Since it was the play's premiering night in Chicago, there were a few cameras outside of the theater. Layla could tell Tony was getting the full effect of hanging out with Dominique.

"This is kind of wild," Tony said to her as they were headed to their balcony seats. "Does he have many normal outings where cameras aren't following him around?" he asked her and she shook her head.

"No, he has to be wearing like a baseball cap and sunglasses or something. Incognito," she told him.

Once they were seated, they got to relax a bit and sit back to enjoy the show. It was absolutely amazing. Layla loved every bit of it. They all enjoyed it actually, even LJ who was very well behaved throughout the show. Afterward, when they went to dinner, LJ was pretty much asleep. It was a great day all in all.

"So do you have practice before the game tomorrow?" she asked Dominique as they were getting into bed. LJ was knocked out in his crib and Tony in the guest bedroom.

"Yeah, I do, have to leave early." He sighed, pulling Layla snug against his chest once they laid down.

"Thanks for the great day we had today," she told him and he simply kissed her shoulder.

"Anything for you," he murmured.

Layla felt as content as she'd ever been falling asleep in his arms.

Come morning, Dominique woke her up early with kisses trailing down her neck. His hands already full of her breasts and his body pressed to hers. She felt his erection against her thigh and reached down to rub the length of him. Before long, he was filling her up and carrying her off to ecstasy. Afterward, she fell asleep quite sated until she woke up a few hours later to start the day.

"Hey, little man." She went to pick up LJ from his crib and Tony joined them.

"Morning..." he said with a yawn. "What are we doing today?" he asked groggily.

"Hanging out with Cliff. I want you guys to meet," she told him and he nodded thoughtfully.

"Okay, that's cool," he said and she asked him to get some coffee going downstairs while she got LJ ready for the day. Afterward, they met Cliff at a nearby café.

"Cliff!" Layla greeted him with a hug and kiss on the cheek, then she introduced him to Tony. "This is my cousin Tony, the one I've been telling you about."

"It's nice to meet you finally. Layla goes on and on about you," Cliff said as he offered his hand for Tony to shake.

"Likewise, she's told me all about you, too," Tony said. "I have to say, it's kind of a relief that you found Layla," he told Cliff.

"It is to me also," Cliff said and Layla felt a little weird about being the topic of conversation.

"So... I mean what's it like to be you?" Tony asked and Layla stifled a laugh.

"Stressful, that's for sure," Cliff laughed. "But it's good to have family that I can unwind with." Cliff smiled at Layla fondly and she grinned in return. "I heard you're doing pretty well for yourself at Cellular."

"Oh yeah. I'm moving up pretty fast there. Sometimes I'm excited, other times I'm sort of worried," Tony said honestly.

"Don't be worried. You're talented and those who have a knack for things always end up exactly where they're supposed to be. Remember that," Cliff said. "Also don't be afraid to settle down. If you find the right woman, don't let her go."

"I'll keep that in mind." Tony chuckled.

Layla was happy to see Cliff sort of taking Tony under his wing, as if he were his son or something. It made her love him all the more. They spent much of the day with Cliff. He gave them a tour of his prototype lab and they saw a lot of cool stuff in the making or already made. It was clear to see how much Cliff really enjoyed what he did.

"So how are things with Dominique?" Cliff asked Layla.

They were just leaving his facility, about to head home though Cliff wouldn't be joining them for the game.

"Oh, you know… they're really good," she said a bit vaguely.

"Has he proposed yet?"

Layla's jaw dropped a little and Tony chuckled on the other side of her.

"What? It's a valid question," Cliff said.

"It is. I mean… I don't see what's taking him so long. He's obviously head over heels," Tony piped up.

"He hasn't proposed yet, no. But I'm fine moving at his pace," Layla insisted.

"Do you see yourself marrying him?" Cliff asked seriously.

"Well, yeah, I do," she said honestly.

"Maybe I should have one of those father-to-potential-son-in-law talks with him," Cliff mused and Layla's jaw did drop then.

"Please don't. That's embarrassing," she said and Tony laughed.

"Hey, I already had one of those big brother talks with Dominique, regardless of the fact that he could wipe the floor with me."

Layla looked at him, wide-eyed. Of course all he did was laugh.

"We're just looking out for you is all," Cliff said, defending Tony.

"Guys, it's unnecessary." She almost pouted, but they ignored her.

After Cliff walked them out, she, Tony, and LJ went back home to get ready for the game.

"Hey, so are we going to sit courtside tonight?" he asked her eagerly. "You know, so you can yell plays at Dominique," he teased and she shoved his arm while he laughed.

"Saw that, did you?" she said with a chuckle.

"Oh yeah, I mean who *didn't*?" he said, still laughing.

"Well, last time, LJ was miserable sitting courtside, so I think we're going to opt for the family booth," she said ruefully.

Anyway, she knew the cameras would be in her face if she sat courtside again. John drove them to the game and she thought it appropriate to ask him what was up with his attitude shift.

"Hey, John...?" He was holding the door open for her to put LJ in his car seat and looked at her expectantly. "What's up with you?" she asked.

"Nothing is up, everything's same old," he said evasively.

"Sure, right. Then how come we don't have our little chats anymore?"

"It's not my place to say, Layla. I haven't been very professional when it came to you, but I'm trying to change that," he said honestly.

"Did Dominique talk to you or something?" she asked and Tony rolled LJ's stroller around to the other passenger side to put him in himself.

"We had a talk, but you have nothing to worry about, it wasn't an argument or anything."

"Are you sure?" she asked him and he nodded once.

"Okay, then... so will you stop acting so weird?"

"Like I said, I'm only trying to be more professional," he said and she sighed.

"You know; I was counting you as my friend. I don't have many in the city…"

His expression wavered then and he sighed.

"Well, I see you as my friend as well, but you know you're with Dominique Johnson. With a word, he can make or break my career and I don't want to get in between you two."

Layla pursed her lips and sighed.

"I'll talk to him," she murmured. "We can still be friends when you're off duty," she said adamantly and John didn't have much of a reply for that.

She got into the car, Tony sitting in the front while she sat in the back with LJ. When they got to the stadium, they went up to the family booth and settled in to watch the game. Dominique actually ran up there minutes before the game just to give Layla and LJ a kiss, which she really loved. Though she did want him to have his head in the game as they were up against the number two team in the east; Chicago was number one. Though that hardly mattered. Their records for wins and losses were virtually the same. Whoever won this game would determine who was number one and who was number two.

"This is exciting," Tony said eagerly and Layla snorted.

He was like a little kid. She held LJ in her lap, though he kept wanting to stretch his legs and stand on her lap. She wondered briefly if he'd walk before even fully crawling.

"I know, my palms are sweaty for him right now," Layla said, causing the person next to her to chuckle.

She glanced over and recognized another player's wife there with their ten-year-old on the other side of her.

"Marge right?" Layla said and she nodded, a friendly smile on Marge's face.

"I'm pretty nervous for them, too, the only reason I'm up here is because I'd be screaming at Cory the whole time he's playing," she chuckled. "And embarrassing my son," she added and Layla chuckled.

"I know for a fact I'd be trying to coach again. That's why I'm not down there," she laughed.

"We're glad you did say something though. They might not have won that game if Dominique didn't make that shot off of stealing the ball," Marge said.

She and Layla chatted some more and Layla found that she really liked Marge. She was genuine and soft spoken. She also reminded Layla a little of Kelly Rippa in resemblance, though a younger, less-skinny version. When the game heated up, though, everyone's attention was on the court. Tony had to hold LJ because Layla was screaming just as much as the other family members in the booth. The game went into overtime and the Horns won by *one* free throw. The stadium was practically a riot the crowd was screaming so loud after their Chicago Horns win.

Layla was practically on a high as if she were one of the players who'd worked hard for that win. She was just that excited for Dominique and the team. Just like every other game she'd been to, she went to the press conference room to wait for Dominique. John and Tony accompanying her. Only when she got to the hallway, more than a few media personnel were outside of the room instead of inside, even though security was trying to corral them in. As soon as they spotted Layla they all rushed over to her, cameras flashing and questions thrown out all at once.

"All of you need to back away. No one's answering any questions."

Through the confusion, she heard John's voice and the stadium security helped move the media where they were supposed to be.

"What was that about?" Layla said as she checked on LJ, making sure his eyes were okay after all the flashing. He was fine—grumpy, but okay.

"You didn't hear the questions?" Tony asked hoarsely.

John came back to them then and told them that they should head back to the car.

"Wait, but…" Layla protested, wanting to stay and wait for Dominique, but he came striding out of the locker room, his expression pissed off.

"Hey, I need you guys to get to my house, pronto," he said, a hand on the small of Layla's back.

"But what's going on?" she asked him and he sighed.

"Look it up, it's all over. A stupid rumor," he said through clenched teeth. "Tony, don't let it affect you, I'll clear this up," he said sincerely and Layla sighed in frustration.

She should have tried to make sense of what was being yelled at them when the media swarmed.

"Go to the car," he told them again as a few stadium security guys showed up to help escort them out.

"Every time I think that shit is in the past…" Tony mumbled to himself as they walked briskly to John's car.

"What happened? What were they saying?" she asked him.

"They were asking if I'd been convicted for drugs before, if I was a part of some South Side gang."

Layla's jaw dropped.

"*What*? How would they know that? Why would they…"

She was baffled and angry that the media would target her cousin in such a way. And for what? Why were they trying to dig up some story on him anyway? They got to John's car and quickly got

237

inside. Soon they were heading home. John drove faster than he usually did. They actually passed by Layla's block and she saw a bunch of paparazzi standing around her front gate.

"Oh my goodness…"

Dominique's house was only a little bit better. They were able to get in easily enough and used the kitchen entrance to get inside. Layla almost immediately went to the family room to turn on the TV and see what was up.

*"Tabloids are popping up all over the place about star basketball player, Dominique Johnson today. Apparently, his new love interest and mother of his son, Lucas Johnson, is involved with an ex-convict. This man, Tony Morrison, was found to have a record involving drugs and leaves people to wonder what he's doing in relation with Johnson. It was just yesterday that these photos were taken of a strangely clandestine meeting with Layla Anderson, Tony, and an unknown man in Chicago's South Side. Notorious for its homicides and criminal activity…"*

The entertainment anchor went on to speculate how Dominique's "involvement" with Tony could jeopardize Dom's career. Layla's heart sank in her chest. She felt horrible that Tony was being targeted. Things were finally going well for him and who knows, his job could be in jeopardy, too. She tuned back to the TV when a picture of Isabelle was shown on the screen.

*"Interest in this is only exacerbated after a not-so-vague tweet from Dominique's ex fiancée Isabelle, saying, 'Sometimes I just hope he learns who he left love for. I hope that he doesn't get hurt.' Now all sorts of speculations are popping up on just who is Layla Anderson and her seemingly only relative Tony Morrison."*

Disgusted, Layla turned the TV off. Of course Isabelle had something to say. She couldn't just leave well enough alone.

"I have to get back to Maryland."

Tony startled her, he was standing just inside the room, Layla hadn't even heard him walk in. He was holding LJ in his arms and rubbing his back.

"Your job called you?" she asked, her throat closing a little with worry and anxiety.

"No, but at least there I can dodge this mess and make sure I don't lose my job," he said morosely.

Layla went over to him and gave him a hard hug.

"I'm sorry, Tony. I'm so sorry," she murmured.

"I'm sorry, too… It seems I can never shake my mistakes as a kid," he said and she heard the hurt in his voice, her own heart squeezing because of his shame and anger.

"Try not to worry too much. Dominique will clear this up. We'll get to the bottom of it," she promised him.

"When do you think we'll be able to get back to your place? So I can get my things?" he asked, handing LJ over to her.

"I'm not sure…" she murmured.

"Layla? Tony?" Dominique finally got there and he found them up in the family room. "Guys, I'm so sorry about this, all of this. Tony, I'm going to make sure you don't get implicated in this anymore," he said sincerely and Layla heard the guilt in his voice, though his facial expression was determined and a little pissed off.

"I have to get back to Maryland, Dom," Tony said and he nodded.

"Yeah, definitely. Don't worry, you'll get there without the media in your face," he said and Layla felt even worse at having her weekend with Tony cut short.

Dominique made quick arrangements to get Tony to the airport and before she knew it she was hugging him goodbye.

"Try not to worry, okay?" she said and he simply nodded, not saying anything. "It'll be okay," she said. When he pulled away, he wouldn't meet her eyes and that bothered her. "Call me when you land," she said and he nodded again. "Tony," she said adamantly and he finally met her eyes.

"Be strong, okay? We weren't raised any other way," she reminded him and he took a deep breath before hugging her tightly again. "I love you," she said fiercely.

"I love you, too," he whispered and then went to go get his things from her house and hit the airport.

"My lawyer is all over this Layla, trust me. No one important believes those tabloids," Dominique said.

"What's your plan?" she asked him, her tone all business.

He paused for a second, his eyes on hers without the cover of his anger at the situation. She saw that he was worried and hoped like hell it wasn't because he thought he couldn't fix things.

# *The Final Chapter*

She didn't trust him. He could tell and he didn't like it. His worst fears were coming true and he didn't want to lose her to them. She and LJ were all he really had, his family. He wouldn't let the damn media, nor fucking Isabelle, get in his way of happiness.

"My lawyer's going to look into these tabloids' sources. He's bound to find lie after lie and I'll bury any media outlet under piles of libel suits if I have to," he promised her. He'd also look into having Tony's record sealed so crap like that wouldn't happen again.

"How fast does your lawyer work?" she asked.

Usually, Layla was so careful not to ask him of anything. Not to be demanding at all, but her family was on the line and he knew she wouldn't be able to rest until the threat was taken care of. He just had to find where all that speculation crap originated.

"As fast as I need him to. Don't worry; he's on it as we speak. Plus, he has a whole team behind him. They'll get to the bottom of it. *We'll* get to the bottom of it," he promised her and she studied him for a moment before nodding slowly.

"So I guess LJ and I are stuck at home again, too, right?" she asked with a sigh.

He hated that she felt like she was feeling. Like a prisoner or something.

"No, I hired some more security. They sent all the paparazzi scattering," he assured her.

His phone buzzed in his pocket with a text. He pulled it out to see it was John, who headed up the security team he pulled together from the agency he worked for. 'Taken care of, I'll leave one of my guys until he boards,' it read. Tony had gotten to the airport safe, thankfully.

"Will I be able to get to work Monday?" she asked, chewing on her bottom lip. Something she did when she was unsure.

"Of course. Please, Layla, don't worry too much," he said, trying to reassure her.

"I'm worried about Tony, he's sensitive..." she said distractedly. "If he loses his job... I don't know... he might backslide," she said, obviously voicing a deep fear of hers.

Dominique slid his phone back into his pocket and pulled her into his arms.

"I need you trust me, please. And also don't leave me," he murmured.

"I'm not going to leave you, Dominique, I just... we have to get this cleaned up," she sighed.

"Trust me," he said again and she nodded her head against his chest.

He glanced over at LJ who was falling asleep in his play pen. It was way past the little guy's bedtime. His phone started vibrating in his pocket again, letting him know it was a call and not just a text. Layla pulled out of his embrace and went over to Lucas. He glanced at his phone's screen and saw it was his lawyer, Daniel, calling.

"I'm going to go feed him and get him ready for bed," Layla said. He nodded then answered the phone.

"So I have good news and upsetting news," Daniel said as soon as Dom answered.

"Upsetting?" he asked.

"The original tabloid article came out after a 'source' sent them on Layla's trail, trying to dig something up on her. Of course, finding her cousin instead with the record of drug possession. That 'source' fueled the tabloid's fire by saying, and I quote, 'the drugs aren't only in his past.'"

"Is that true?" Dominique asked through clenched teeth, wondering who the hell this source was.

"No, it's absolute lies. The company Tony is working for does routine drug tests and even so, he's been clean after going through rehab while serving his short time in prison."

"So who's the source, Daniel?" Dom asked.

"We haven't gotten to the bottom of that yet, but the best route to garner who the source is, is by hitting the tabloid with lawsuits about what they printed. They also got a little bold talking about you wanting to gain street cred by associating with Tony who is 'suspected' to have gang ties. It's a whole fucking mess. I'm actually surprised the tabloid doesn't know any better," Daniel said with disgust in his tone.

"They must really be sure most of it is true…" Dominique mused. He hurried downstairs and grabbed his car keys. He sent a quick text to John to see if Tony was still at the airport.

"That's what I'm having checked out as we speak. We have to be sure. So as for the good news, Layla's clean in all this, completely innocent. I'm getting the lawsuit drawn up for her sake as we speak. Though Clifford Anderson has his own lawyers on top of libel suits, so I'm thinking it would be a good idea to let his guys handle it."

"All right, keep digging for that source… and have someone look into Isabelle's activity. She sent out a tweet that is just nagging at me. I suspect she's who might have tipped off the media in the first place," Dom said.

He ended the call with Daniel a second later and checked his phone. Tony was still in the airport. Dominique had no trouble getting from his place to O'Hare. He managed to talk his way through to the gate of Tony's flight without having to buy a ticket, though he did have to go through extra security checks. He found Tony slouched in a chair, waiting for the flight to be called.

"Tony," Dominique called his attention and he looked up, startled to see Dom there.

"Hey, what are you doin' here?" he asked, confused. "Is everything all right?" he asked, concerned.

Tony really was a good guy; Dominique would be shocked to learn that he was mixed up in anything gang or drug related.

"I just need to talk to you, man-to-man," Dominique said and gestured for Tony to follow him away from other folks waiting for their flight. Thankfully, Dominique's hoodie hid his face enough that no one seemed to notice him other for the fact that he was tall. "I just have to know if you're into anything shady. For the sake of my trying to help you out and get this all over with," Dom said and Tony shook his head before he even finished speaking.

"Of course not, Dom. I finally have good shit going for me, I wouldn't mess any of that up. You gotta believe me, I'm not into anything illegal, *anything*," Tony said with fierce conviction.

Dom saw in his eyes that he was telling the truth. Plus, there was all the circumstantial stuff, like his moving to Maryland.

"I just had to know, to make sure. I'm sorry, man." Dom said and clapped Tony on the shoulder reassuringly.

"I just hate that this crap is affecting me again…" Tony mumbled morosely. "Affecting you, Layla, LJ."

246

The guy was riddled with guilt. Dom knew he was blaming himself just as Dom was feeling he was responsible. Hell, should he have been a normal guy, none of that would be happening.

"It won't for long, man. I'm gonna have your record sealed and shut the media up," Dom promised him again. "No one messes with my family," he added and Tony looked up at him, shocked.

"You'd call *me* family?" he asked in disbelief.

"Of course. You're practically Layla's brother and LJ adores you. Plus, you're a good guy. You're family, man," Dominique said and they hugged it out, as men sometimes do.

"Thanks, Dominique... You don't know how much this means to me," Tony said, emotion heavy in his voice and gaze.

"It'll be over soon, just hang in there," he told Tony and he nodded.

He said his goodbyes to Tony and then was escorted back to his car by airport security. When Dom got back home, he looked for Layla and found her watching the damn news. He was relieved, though, that she was in his bed at least.

"Don't torture yourself," he said, startling her.

"I can't help it... it's like having to watch a freaking car crash."

He walked over to the bed and slipped the remote from her fingers to change the channel.

"Where did you go?" she asked him.

"To talk to Tony," he answered truthfully.

"Is he not at the airport?" She seemed confused and about a second away from worrying again.

"Yes, he's at the airport. Should be boarding soon, don't worry," he assured her. "I just wanted to make sure of a few things is all," he said slowly.

"Like what? You don't believe what any of these things are saying do you?" She looked at him almost accusingly and he sighed.

"No, I just had to make sure, for practical reasons, Layla. We need to have all our bases covered. Did you talk to your dad?"

"Yeah, he called. Said he won't let the media talk about me and Tony like they are. He wants you to call him," she said and rubbed her eyes.

Only then did Dom realize her eyes were red and a bit puffy.

"Have you been crying over this?" he asked her, getting into bed and pulling her against his chest.

She had her curly hair up in a bun and was wearing one of his t-shirts that he usually wore around the house.

"I know it's silly, but I mean—things have been good," she said he hugged her tighter to his chest.

"They will be again, I'll make things like they were," he said. "I'll find out who's behind all this."

"It's Isabelle," she mumbled.

"I have a feeling it is, too, but I have to be sure before confronting her in any way," he said.

"What if we're right?"

Dom took a deep breath and inhaled Layla's clean scent. Her hair smelled like fruit and the rest of her like that soap she always used that reminded him of caramel and vanilla.

"Then I'll deal with her. If she won't leave us alone, I'll be the one to drag her name through the mud."

His tone was hard; he'd had enough of Isabelle. He tilted Layla's head up so that he could kiss her, needing the reassurance of her love and acceptance of him, even though he brought nothing but craziness into her life. He slid his hand underneath the blanket, finding her without any bottoms on apart from panties. She took a deep breath and he kissed her neck, trying to get her to relax some.

"Dom, I don't really feel like it tonight," she said and small pang went through him, instantly making him worried, worried that she was pulling away from him.

"What can I do?" he asked, his voice a bit hoarse, less from lust and more from his hoping like hell she wouldn't leave him once he cleared everything up with the whole Tony thing.

"You're already doing it," she assured him. She looked into his eyes, hers the prettiest shade of brown he'd ever seen. It often reminded him of molten caramel. Sometimes he wished LJ had gotten her eyes instead of his. "I'm just tired and a little emotionally…spent," she said.

"Are you sure?" he asked her, almost anxiously and wondering if she saw right through him.

"Yes, I'm sure."

She studied him closely for a second and then sighed a little and climbed onto his lap, straddling him. She took his face in her hands and kissed him soundly on the lips. He circled her waist with his hands and pulled her back with him until his back rested against the headboard. She rocked against his erection as she felt it press up against her core. She tangled her fingers in his hair, pulling on it a little, which he loved. He licked into her mouth, she tasted like mint. Her previous statement about not being in the mood was forgotten, especially as he grabbed her full round ass in his hands and squeezed. A breathy moan escaped her lips and he slid his mouth down to her neck, biting her skin, bolstering her cries of pleasure.

Dom was hard as a rock and all they were doing was making out. He wanted to be inside of her more than he needed his next breath. She slid her hands underneath his shirt, her fingers splayed across his pecs. She ran her hands up to his neck and back down to his stomach. He let out an almost-pained moan, he loved it when she touched him like that, as if he were everything she wanted. She pushed his shirt over his head and trailed kisses across his chest. She inched off of his lap to undo his fly and she gingerly freed his erection from his pants. Before he could even get the damn confining things off, her mouth was around his cock and he hissed as she took him deep. He had to hold himself in check so that he wouldn't cause her to gag too much, but damn if she didn't cause his toes to curl. Almost every muscle in his body was taut with the need to come, she circled her tongue around the sensitive head and took him to the back of her throat again.

"Fuck, Layla," he groaned and couldn't help swiveling his hips.

His cock was hard as a rock and he was about seconds away from releasing into her mouth. She sucked hard on the tip of his cock and he practically exploded, his whole body shuddering with the orgasm as he shot into her mouth.

"Ah…" he stroked himself, pumping every last bit into her mouth and she drank it all.

Layla sat back on her heels, and he moved forward, forcing her to lie back so he could slip her panties off. He got the rest of his clothes off clumsily and found her smirking at him.

"I'm not going anywhere…" she said shyly and he smiled.

"I hope not," he said, more serious than he intended to be.

Her expression sobered a bit and understanding crossed her features. She opened her arms to him and he went. Kissing her softly and pressing his body against hers, feeling her warmth. He wanted to be inside her, but he'd make sure to take care of her just as she did for him. He slid down to settle in between her legs and she opened up for him. He delved right in, licking into her core and sucking on her clit. She cried out, her chest heaving with every pant and her legs trembling on his shoulders and back. When he slid one finger into her tight and silky heat, he felt her clench around it and groaned against her sensitive flesh. He wasn't sure if he could hold out until she climaxed. She was already soaking wet; he could practically drink her up. He quickly moved up, kneeling in front of her and angled her hips so that he could slide into her.

She sighed at the same time he did, he was home. Whenever he was one with Layla, he felt utterly at home. He lowered his torso to hers, holding himself up on his forearms as he moved his hips. He knew exactly how she liked things and had her clawing at his back and crying out his name in no time. All the while she pulsed and clenched around his sex, making it impossible for him not to climax almost as many times as she did.

Dominique felt weak by the time Layla passed out, his joints very loose and his head a little light. He checked the time and took a quick shower before trying Cliff, it was nearly midnight. He hoped he could get through to him.

"Dominique, I've been waiting for your call." Cliff answered on the second ring.

"Hey, Cliff, sorry I've just been handling a few things," he replied.

"I understand and this should be quick, but I think it's a good idea if we try to strategize our legal teams, so we don't clash lawsuits."

"Well, my team is more focused on the media, trying to find that source of theirs and take that tabloid down. Also, I was going to try and have Tony's record sealed."

Dom stood next to the bed, watching Layla sleep. The sight of her naked and all tangled in his sheets always did something to his chest, made it all full and tight at the same time.

"Let me handle the lawsuits for Layla's name as well as Tony's and I'll see about getting his record sealed. You have your lawyers focus on the tabloid. I don't want to see *The Star Gazette* even on Google searches," Cliff said with disgust when he mentioned the tabloid that started it all.

"Will do," Dom said and promised to let Daniel know to cooperate with Cliff's lawyers on all of it as well.

"Take care of her, Dominique," Cliff said, a clear warning in his tone.

Dominique knew that especially with Cliff in her life, Layla could seriously leave him if she had enough of the craziness that was the constant media presence he brought into her life.

"I will, Cliff," he said sincerely and they ended the call shortly after.

Dominique had a lot of respect for Cliff, he came into Layla's life right when she needed her own family around her. He balanced out Dominique's fully entering her life. Before he climbed into bed behind Layla he went to check on LJ, who was actually wide awake and playing with the few toys in his crib with him.

"What are you doing up, little man?" He bent down to pick him up. Lucas was getting taller and gaining some more weight. Soon he wouldn't be a baby anymore. LJ stared up at Dom with his big green eyes, a mirror of Dom's own. "You're supposed to be asleep," he said and LJ yawned. "Yeah, I know… Sometimes I wake up in the middle of the night, too," he said and kissed LJ on the forehead. He yawned again and his eyelids drooped. Dominique kept talking to him, telling him how much he loved him until LJ was fast asleep. He gingerly settled him into bed before tiptoeing back to Layla.

He turned off the TV and sent a text to Daniel, updating him on what he was to focus on. Afterward, he put his phone to charge and shut off the lamp light. He curled around Layla and held her close to him. He never wanted to let go.

\*\*\*

Come morning, both Dom and Layla were woken up to LJ's crying. He'd never heard Lucas so upset and ran just as fast as Layla to go check on him. She picked him up out of his crib and made a tsking sound.

"He has a fever," she said and looked at him with concern as she took him to the changing table and pulled out the baby thermometer. "Shh, don't worry we'll make it okay, baby boy." She tried consoling him, but he wasn't having it.

"He's one-oh-one," Dom said as he tilted his head to look at the thermometer.

"Can you try feeding him while I call the pediatrician?" she asked him and he nodded.

He quickly checked LJ's diaper, since he was already there and did a change before taking him downstairs to warm up a bottle for him. He grabbed his phone to Google baby fevers, his chest tight from LJ crying so hard. Hell, he wanted to cry, if he could take away his fever, he would in a heartbeat.

"It's all right, we'll get you better, little man," he murmured while trying to get LJ to calm down a little.

As he waited for a bottle of breast milk to warm up he checked his phone and saw a text from Daniel. "It was her," was all it said and for a second Dominique saw red. He took several deep breaths, remembering that he first had to make sure LJ was all right before going after his ex to confront her. He was just about to sit down to feed him when Layla came hurrying downstairs.

"What did the doctor say?" he asked her and she fixed her robe as she walked over to a still crying LJ.

"If he doesn't stop crying and doesn't eat, we have to take him to the hospital," she said, her voice oddly calm even though what she just said scared the shit out of Dominique.

"The hospital?" he asked, trying to keep his voice level for LJ's sake.

She simply nodded and held her hands out for Lucas. Dominque passed him over, along with the bottle. He held his breath as Layla struggled to try and get him to eat. After about ten tense minutes of coaxing him to eat, Layla decided to give him a lukewarm bath. He did calm down a bit after that and even ate some. Dominique breathed a sigh of relief only when he saw Layla do so.

"Should we still take him, just to be sure?" Dom asked her anxiously.

"After he eats, I'll check his temperature again. If it's dropped, we simply have to make sure he doesn't get another one. But he'll have to go see the pediatrician soon anyway," she said. "I made an appointment with him for later this afternoon, that's if we don't have to take LJ to the hospital beforehand. He'll make a house call. He was really nice about everything," she said in a soft voice.

LJ was staring up at her unwaveringly, water still in his eyes from crying. Dominique found it a good sign that he had tears. Hopefully, it was just a passing thing.

"So the doctor is coming either way?" Dom had to make sure and she nodded.

"Yeah, he is," she said and glanced down at LJ when he reached up to his ear and started to fuss.

Dominique bent down to press a kiss to LJ's forehead, which was still a bit warm.

"So I'm going to file a lawsuit for slander against Isabelle." He sighed, sitting down next to them on the couch.

"It was her?" Layla asked with wide eyes.

"Yeah, I don't know the specifics yet though," he told her.

"So… you're going to make the lawsuit public?" she asked him slowly.

"Of course. She put us through hell," he said adamantly.

"Well, maybe we can meet with her and try to get her to leave us alone once and for all."

Layla blew Dominique's mind. How was she willing to put everything Isabelle put her through, *them* through, behind her? Hell, Dom could even circumstantially pin LJ's fever on Isabelle.

"You want to try and *reason* with that?" he asked incredulously.

"Yes, I do. If we just lash out at her, she'll only hit back and I don't want to be stuck in some cycle until she finally moves on when LJ is, like, twenty and we have two other kids."

Dom smiled then. The only thing on his mind was what she just said. She saw a future with him and hell if that didn't make him want to give her everything under the sun.

"Fine, how about this?" He paused to kiss her soundly on the lips and she gave him a small smile. "I still draw up the lawsuit and we set up a meeting and threaten to go through with it, making it public. I don't think anything is more precious to her at the moment than her career and her name."

"Okay… that's fair," she said and bounced LJ in her lap, trying to burp him, but he was already hiccupping and fussing.

"Let me try with him. Why don't you got put some clothes on so the doctor doesn't come here and catch sight of your boobs. I wouldn't want to have to knock him out," he told her and she smiled again.

She passed LJ over and gave him a sound kiss before caressing Dom's chin and heading toward the stairs. He needed to get dressed as well; he was only in a pair of boxers.

"How about we turn on a fan for you, will that be better?" he told LJ, who simply wailed and put his thumb in his mouth. Dom stood up and turned on the fan. Once the air in the room started to circulate a little, he quieted even more. "It's your ear, isn't it?" he guessed and pressed his hand against LJ's ears, they were hotter than the rest of him. "I wonder if I can put some ice around your ear…"

he mused while fanning LJ's head. He really liked that; it calmed him down even more.

"Oh my goodness, you got him to stop fussing," Layla said as she hurried back downstairs, wearing a pair of winter tights and a long sweater. Her hair was out, all curly and tumbling over her shoulders.

Dom still couldn't believe he lucked out with such a perfect woman.

"I think he has an ear infection. His ears are hot," he said.

"Both of them?" she asked and he nodded.

Dom passed LJ over to Layla who blew on his ears. He went to find one of those little handheld fans he knew he had. He got one for Layla and she laughed when LJ practically sighed in relief once she started fanning his ears.

"Poor baby," she said and kissed LJ on the forehead.

Dominique went to go change and wait for the doctor to arrive before he went to visit Daniel and see what he'd gotten done. He definitely owed the guy a bonus for working day and night. They both hung around, fanning LJ's ears until Dr. Peters rang the doorbell. Dom went to answer it, shaking the doctor's hand and inviting him inside.

"Hey, Dr. Peters, thanks for coming on such short notice."

"Of course, it's what I do," he said. "Now, where's baby Lucas?" he asked and Dom led him to the family room.

"Just on an educated guess here, I'm going to say he has an ear infection," Peters said as he walked into the room, seeing Layla fanning LJ's ears.

"Yeah, we think it might be," she said with a sheepish chuckle.

Peters took LJ and laid him down on his play blanket. He opened up his doctor's bag and first checked his temperature and then his ears.

"Well, he's still running a temperature, and he does have quite a nasty infection in the right ear. The left ear is a little better. I'm going to have to do a flush. This won't be pleasant for him," Peters said and Layla was right there seeing how she could help.

Dom had no choice but to hover in the background as Peters got ready flush LJ's ears of whatever was in there. Even Dom cringed when he saw what Peters was doing. Layla had to help hold LJ's head over a little basin. He screamed to holy hell when the doctor flushed his ears and Dom cringed when he saw the giant yellow infection fall out of his ear.

"That was *in* there?" Dom asked, shocked.

"Yep. That infection would make anyone cry," Peters said. "I'm going to leave you with drops to put in both his ears, two in the left, one in the right before he goes to sleep at night and in the morning. You'll need to hold the drops in there with a bit of cotton…"

Dom listened to the instructions the doctor gave and he demonstrated with LJ's first dose.

"The drops should help with some of his discomfort as well. Should his ears get hot, just run a wash cloth under cool water and put them over his ears. No need to sit there and fan him." He chuckled. After a few more instructions, Dom saw him out and took a breath of relief.

"So just an ear infection, thank God." Dominique sighed. LJ was falling asleep, pooped from his fever and being worked on by the doctor.

"I'm going to put him to bed, watch him for a while," she said and Dom nodded, kissing both she and LJ as they got up.

"I've got to go and visit Daniel. Have you spoken to Tony today?"

"Yeah, he sent a text that he got in okay, I'll give him a call once LJ is asleep."

"All right, I'll see you soon," he said and went to grab his keys to head over to River North.

He called Daniel once he was closer to his office.

"Hey Dom, I've got an update for you, but it's quite a bit of information. You might want to come in so we can lay everything out."

"I'm on the way right now, actually, just making sure you were in," he said and Daniel said he'd see him when he got there.

Cliff called him as soon as he ended the call with Daniel.

"Hey, are you near Layla? I just tried calling her," he said when Dom answered the call.

"No, LJ woke up with a bad ear infection. The doctor just left the house so she's been seeing to him. She might be on the phone with Tony or something, too," Dom filled him in.

"Well, I wanted to update her on things. My lawyers were able to get retractions and even a few apologies for her and Tony. Everyone's settling rather than paying the costs I'm throwing at them," he said smugly.

"Wow, your guys work *fast*," Dom said appreciatively.

"Yep, and now they're working on sealing Tony's record. How're your guys coming along?"

"I'm heading to my lawyer's office now. He said he had some updates for me. But he knows for sure that the source was Isabelle."

"Are you going to handle it?" Cliff asked.

"I am—well I *want to*. But Layla wants to try and be diplomatic. I'll draw up the slander lawsuit and only go public with it if she doesn't cooperate in leaving us alone. Layla wants to… talk to her," he said.

Cliff paused, then he laughed.

"That sounds exactly like her. Keep me posted," he said briskly and ended the call.

Dom rode the rest of the way in silence. When he got to Daniel's office, he was shown to the law firm's conference room where Daniel was situated with a team of four guys. Papers were strewn across the long conference table as well as tablets and laptops. They'd been busy at work.

"You guys went above and beyond," Dom said when he stepped into the room.

"Dominique, hey, good to see you, man," Daniel greeted him with a handshake and he went around the room shaking everyone's hand.

"So take a seat. We'll lay everything out for you."

Dom sat down in one of the comfortable swivel chairs and leaned back.

"All right, we had to go through backdoor everything to find a weak staffer at *Star Gazette* who gave up their famous source. He said it was indeed Isabelle and we have the proof to back up his claims. But that's minutia. The big kickers are the fact that she hired that photographer to follow Layla around the day Tony came in from the airport. That's *begging* for a larger lawsuit. We could carry everything on a harassment suit. It's a bit of a stretch at places, but essentially she orchestrated your misery." Daniel went on a bit while Dominique ground his teeth, his anger mounting.

"Stop, I don't want to hear about Isabelle anymore, what about *The Gazette?*"

"Well, we're already set to bury them in libel suits, otherwise they'll have to print the biggest retraction and try to save face by revealing Isabelle as their source, being the origin of a scandal getting out to help their credibility…"

For some reason, that didn't sit well with Dominique, even if he was beyond pissed off with her. He didn't want her to be absolutely ruined by having what she did come to light.

"Draw up the lawsuit against Isabelle, but don't file anything for court unless I say. On the other hand, can you find a way to make sure that tabloid doesn't even have a history off of this?"

"We can draw up some avenues, go on corruption since they took a bribe like tip…"

"Actually, they *did* take a bribe since Isabelle paid one of their own photographers to follow Layla Anderson around," one of the other lawyers said.

"Sounds like you all have more brainstorming to do then," Dominique said as he got up.

"All right so, draw up the lawsuit, don't file it. I'll fax that to you ASAP, then we'll get to work on taking *Gazette* to court and getting them shut down. It'll take a little bit of time, but we'll make it happen without a doubt."

Daniel wrote down his orders and Dom thanked everyone for their hard work before he left. By the time he got back to the house, Daniel had sent him everything. It was all neatly printed in his office. He put everything in a scary looking manila folder. People usually feared things handed to them in a manila folder if they didn't know what it was.

"Hey…" he glanced back and saw Layla standing in the doorway, a curious smile on her face.

"Got the papers drawn up to threaten Isabelle with. How's LJ? Have you spoken to your dad?" He fired the questions at her as they ran through his mind and she giggled at him.

She walked into the room and wrapped her arms around his waist.

"LJ is napping. His temperature is back to normal and his ears aren't bothering him for now. Yes, I spoke to Cliff and I'm beyond relieved and blown away that he handled things so quickly. That you both jumped on things so fast."

Dom smiled and wrapped his arms around her tight.

"So what do you say? You want to call Nadia over for an hour and pop in on the popstar diva?" he asked her, making her laugh again.

"Sure, but we have to be back in an hour. I don't want to be away from him too long and he's sick," she said while dialing Nadia's number.

Thankfully, she was available on late notice. Nadia was over in under ten minutes and Layla took another ten to give Nadia the complete rundown on LJ, though Dominique knew for a fact the nanny has seen an ear infection or twenty in her time. He had to give her props, she listened to Layla and didn't act at all superior. She was a really good nanny.

"So do you know where she is?" Layla asked as Dominique drove to Isabelle's penthouse in Greektown.

"If she's not home then we'll try the recording studio. She has this thing about routine. If she's not on tour or interviewing, she'll be in either of those two places."

Dominique left out the bits about her gym times and the restaurants she frequents for breakfast, lunch, or dinner. Layla didn't need to know the boring details he picked up on Isabelle over time.

"So what if she's interviewing?" Layla asked slowly, he could feel her gaze on him.

"I'm not calling her," he said, his hand tightening on the wheel.

"You don't have to be nice, but I mean… what if she's naked?" Layla asked, causing Dominique to suddenly crack up into laughter.

"Fine… I'll—fine." He sighed and called Isabelle's cell.

"Look who's calling as soon as he hears the truth."

She answered on the first ring, sounding all fucking smug. His phone was hooked up to the car's Bluetooth. Layla heard every hateful word.

"Yeah… look, I want to talk to you. Are you home?"

"Home, yeah, I'm home," she chuckled.

Dominique couldn't believe he asked someone so manipulative and crazy to marry him. He shook his head and ended the call.

"I think I'll need a drink after this." He sighed and Layla nodded in agreement.

When they got to Isabelle's building, Dominique didn't have to wait for security to call up. He was able to go ahead with Layla in tow. When the elevator opened up to the marble foyer, Isabelle's welcoming smirk soured instantly into a scowl when she saw Layla.

"What are *you* doing here?" she practically snarled.

She was wearing a tight sweater dress and heels. A long time ago that might have appealed to Dominique, but he only had attraction for Layla.

"We're here to talk, and I'd be nice to Layla if I were you. She's the only reason I'm not going public with this lawsuit and seriously hurting your career right now," he practically growled at her.

Isabelle glanced down at the hand that held the folder; her eyes did widen then and he took satisfaction in her manila fear.

"Fine," she said in a clipped tone and gestured for them to follow her into the living room.

She sat down on the couch and Layla took a seat across from her on the loveseat. Dominique remained standing.

"I need you to understand that I love Layla and I love my son. The fact that you started all of this mess, almost ruined her cousin's life and dragged our names through the mud, is *unacceptable*. You'd better stop this vengeance crap right now or it'll get really tough for you very soon."

Dominique's tone was absolute and there was a brief silence as Isabelle stared at him in disbelief.

"You barely even *know* her," she insisted.

"I know her a lot better than I knew you," he said honestly.

"Look… Isabelle, we don't want to get stuck in some cycle of hurting each other. I have a son. Lucas is only four months old and all of this affects him, too. Lashing out at me or Dominique has more implications than you think."

Isabelle turned her gaze to Layla and simply blinked at her a few times.

"Do you get it? That I have a family now and things are done between us."

Dominique pulled her attention back to him and she took a deep shuddering breath.

"I'm sorry," she whispered.

Both Dom and Layla were practically flabbergasted that she was apologizing out of all the possible characteristic responses.

"You have a baby and he's innocent," she admitted. "For that, I'm sorry."

Dominique recovered. It made sense that was the only thing she was apologizing for.

"Will you let us be?" he asked her.

"Will you file that lawsuit?" she fired back, but with less conviction. At least she felt remorseful.

"I won't, but that doesn't mean that I can't at any time," he warned.

"Whatever… it's fine. We're done, I get it," she said and stood up, her eyes downcast though she always held her head up.

Dominique felt he should apologize for how things ended, smooth things out between them a bit further, but she didn't deserve it. She didn't deserve Layla's kindness. What she got was a gift.

Layla stood up and followed Dominique back to the elevator, they left the manila folder on Isabelle's coffee table.

"Goodbye, Isabelle," he said for emphasis.

"Bye, Dominique," she said softly and the elevator doors opened on cue.

When he and Layla got back to the car, he felt a sudden relief. He felt as if things would finally be over with Isabelle.

"Hey…" he glanced down over at Layla once they were in the car and she smiled softly at him. "I love you, too."

He smiled at her fondly and took her hands in his, kissing her knuckles.

"I think we need a vacation. Somewhere tropical," he said as he started up the engine.

"I couldn't agree more." She chuckled. "Maybe on one of your weekends off?"

"It's a plan," he said and then glanced at her with a private smile. He could wait until they went on the trip, with the romantic setting and the ocean right next to them. But he couldn't wait. He needed to make sure right then and there. "Hey will you marry me?" he asked casually and she did a double take.

"What…? Did you ask if I would…?" she trailed off, her face full of adorable confusion.

"Marry me," he said, his tone more serious and his gaze locked with hers. "You're the one for me, the *only* one and I want to spend the rest of my life with you. *You*." It took her a second, but she recovered, her eyes tearing up a little.

"Of course I'll marry you… of course," she said, her tone and expression saying, "as if there would be any other answer."

A bright and warm joy spread throughout his chest then and he suddenly couldn't sit still. He left the car in park and got out to go and pull Layla out into a bear hug. She laughed as he twirled her around, corny like in the movies. But damn him if he cared. He had the one he needed and he wasn't letting go.

# THE END

**Authors Personal Message:**

**Hey gorgeous!**

**I really hope you enjoyed my novel and if you want to see all my other Pregnancy romances that you can <u>see them all on my Amazon page here</u> :)**

*Thanks in advance*

*Tasha Blue*

# Fancy A FREE BWWM Romance Book??

Join the "**Romance Recommended**" Mailing list today and gain access to an exclusive **FREE** classic BWWM Romance book along with many others more to come. You will also be kept up to date on the best book deals in the future on the hottest new BWWM Romances.

**\* Get FREE Romance Books For Your Kindle & Other Cool giveaways**

**\* Discover Exclusive Deals & Discounts Before Anyone Else!**

**\* Be The FIRST To Know about Hot New Releases From Your Favorite Authors**

Click The Link Below To Access This Now!

## *Oh Yes! Sign Me Up To Romance Recommended For FREE!*

Already subscribed?
OK, Read On!

# A MUST HAVE!

## BABY SHOWER

## 10 BOOK PREGNANCY ROMANCE BOXSET

### 50% DISCOUNT!!

An amazing chance to own 10 complete books for one LOW price!

This package features some of the biggest selling authors from the world of Pregnancy Romance. They have collaborated to bring you this super-sized portion of love, sex and romance involving the drama of a baby on the way!

1 - Tasha Blue – The Best Man's Baby
2 - Alexis Gold – The Movie Star's Designer Baby
3 - Cherry Kay – The Tycoon's Convenient Baby
4 - CJ Howard – The Billionaire's Love Child
5 - Kimmy Love – Her Bosses Baby?
6 - Lacey Legend – The Billionaire's Unwanted Baby
7 - Lena Skye – A Baby Of Convenience
8 - Monica Castle – The Cowboy's Secret Baby
9 - Tasha Blue – Fireman's Baby
10 -Alexis Gold – The Billionaire's Secret Baby

**START READING THIS NOW AT THE BELOW LINKS**

Amazon.com > http://www.amazon.com/The-Baby-Shower-Pregnancy-Billionaires-ebook/dp/B01A5DEUP2

Amazon.co.uk > http://www.amazon.co.uk/The-Baby-Shower-

Pregnancy-Billionaires-ebook/dp/B01A5DEUP2

Amazon.ca > http://www.amazon.ca/The-Baby-Shower-Pregnancy-Billionaires-ebook/dp/B01A5DEUP2

Amazon.com.au > http://www.amazon.com.au/The-Baby-Shower-Pregnancy-Billionaires-ebook/dp/B01A5DEUP2

CPSIA information can be obtained
at www.ICGtesting.com
Printed in the USA
LVOW10s2033050217

523261LV00016B/1060/P